For Mom, Dad, and Ellie,
my first readers

And for Caitlin O'Connell,
adviser, editor extraordinaire, friend

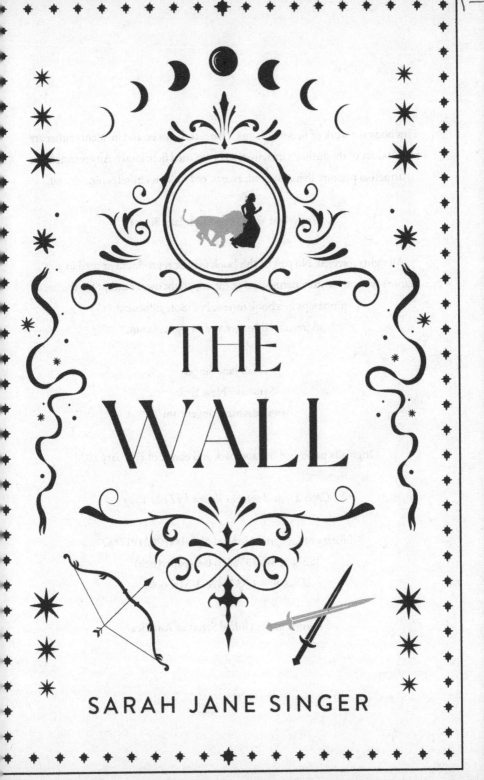

THE
WALL

SARAH JANE SINGER

Sarah Jane Singer
Syracuse, New York
www.sarahjanesinger.com

Originally published in paperback and ebook in February 2022

Cover art and interior design by Lena Yang

Library of Congress Control Number: 2021917882
ISBN 978-1-7378426-0-6 (paperback)
ISBN 978-1-7378426-1-3 (ebook)

Printed in the United States of America

* * ✳ * *

CHAPTER ONE

* * ✳ * *

When I was born, my father built the Wall. My mother cradled me and watched as stone after stone was set, until a great, snow-white wall towered over us, shining like the birches of the forest it kept out. When I was seven, my baby sister was born, and ivy had begun to twine up the face of the Wall, reaching toward the heavens until it realized that all there was above it was more wall, and it crawled over the top of the shining stone and down the other side. When I was ten, my sister died. The Wall was dusky and silent. My mother grew silent as well.

Mother was very much like the Wall. Her porcelain skin shimmered with glossy tears like white stones in the rain, and her sad, green eyes gazed out like emeralds, like the hopeless ivy. She was silent and strong like the Wall, too. Through her illness and her sadness, Mother was the Wall.

At eleven, I clambered up the ivy that twined its way heavenward, and I fell. It felt like floating when I hit the ground. I saw the murky sky as if through the surface of the little pond I'd swum in when I was smaller. Father picked me up gently and carried me inside. He told me, not for the first time, that I was never to climb the Wall again, and I was also never to cross it, never to set foot on the other side. I swore to him I never would, and that I would try better to keep my promises. By the next day, the groundskeepers were tearing the ivy from the Wall, and I could climb no longer.

When I was thirteen, a battered boy near my own age rode through the Wall's tall, solitary gate on a great golden beast. The boy was dark-skinned and beautiful; his beast was exotic and noble, and shimmered in the sunlight like gold thread on a tapestry. My father treated the boy well but did not allow me to speak to him. Boy and beast left after two days. A fortnight later, another beast came through the Wall's heavy gate. No boy accompanied this smaller golden creature; the animal was intended for me. Its mane was adorned with a pink ribbon, and a pink saddle sat upon its short, stocky body. The boy must have sent it. Poor thing. How was he to know I had never liked pink?

Father called the magnificent creature a lion but would let me nowhere near it at first. It was quite apparent, however, that the thing wanted me. It would nudge my hand if I got close to it in its stables, and when my father let it roam the grounds, it would sit patiently beneath my window, making the loveliest sound of pure contentment. I named the lion Zav—gold. Soon, Father relented and let me ride Zav around the grounds like a princess upon a golden mare.

At fourteen, I learned I was not a princess. I had been convinced I was, for weren't princesses the ones who were always hidden from the world in some quiet wonderland, protected by Wall and Father, never to see the outside world? No, Father told me. Those were only storybooks. I learned the difference.

The Wall never seemed like a prison to me, until it did. I suppose it had something to do with growing up or growing restless, but it suddenly seemed the Wall was holding me from something, or someone. I had never known the outside world, but I painted it in my mind, from the stories told by visiting lords and ladies, merchants and traders. There were gray birch trees shimmering with silver thread, a deep blue lake in the clearing of a forest, violets that grew along the wood's path. Those things called to me. And something else called with them: the Lion Boy. The noble boy whose face my mind often dwelled upon, though I could no longer recall it clearly. It was curiosity, I supposed. Where was he from? Did he have a family? Was he some sort of royalty? Did he have a Wall?

From the tower in our manor, I could see over the Wall. A sea of amethyst and emerald trees flooded my vision. The trees spanned miles on all sides, until, startled, they halted, and bowed down before the great white mountain peaks to the north.

North. What beings dwelled there in the wintry halls of the tall mountains? At times, I imagined I could see shining white horses cantering through the snow on the distant mountain tops. I could never tell if they were truly there, or if they were simply flurries of snow that took shape in my mind.

Of course, I always wondered what else there was beyond the horizon. I knew the world was not all forest and mountains. I knew from my father's books and charts that there were villages and towns and markets and great cities. Maps and illustrations were all well and good, but they were not the same as *seeing*.

For so long, though, my father had told me that the Outside was dangerous. He said that he and my mother could not bear to lose me. I had seen what losing my sister had done to my mother, so I stayed. In any case, the great gate of the Wall was sealed. Though it was not locked, it took three grown men to push it open when visitors came. I did not have the strength. Not for the gate, and not to break my mother's heart.

Now I am eighteen. The Wall has stood for as many years, watching my steps, knowing my heart, dreaming my dreams. The Wall holds me captive.

One night, I dreamed of the Outside. It was murky, like my vision after the fall, like a smudge of gray sky after rain, like my mother's tears. All I knew was the Wall with its torn-away ivy. Even in dreams, my mind could not paint a clear picture of what lay beyond it. But though the dream that night would not resolve itself in my mind, the call that came with it was clear. *Go,* it said. *Go out. Something awaits you.*

I woke in the night, sweating and shaking, feeling the pull of the Outside so strongly that my body actually strained toward the high window of my bedroom. Sleep did not find me again that night.

The next morning, my father called me to his study. I thought perhaps we would build another bottled ship together, as we so often did, or perhaps he would read to me from one of his many history books. But instead, he bade me sit and gazed at me solemnly. My father was often solemn, but today seemed different.

"My dear heart," he said, and perhaps it was my imagination, but I thought I heard his voice break, as though he might weep. "I have been summoned. By the Council. They are in need of a merchant with my ... experience." He said the last word bitterly.

"The *Council*?" Of course, I knew of the Council. Even a girl within a Wall knew of the powerful leaders of our realm. My father had sailed for them many years ago, long before I was born. They had made him a lord. He was beholden to them. "But ... we do not leave the Wall."

He took my hands in his, and I felt the warmth, the roughness of his calluses. "That is why I must speak with you today. The Council insists it must be me. No other knows the waters we must sail as I do, they say. No other has traded with the people I must trade with. I must not refuse them. But darling, you must promise me. You must *swear*. While I am gone, you must remain within the Wall."

It was then that I knew I had to leave.

It could not be a coincidence, I thought—the Council's summons, my dream. My father had not left the Wall since before my sister's death. His leaving now had to be by design. I did not want to break my promise or to betray him. But we had had fewer and fewer visitors as the years stretched on. I was tired of looking out over the Wall to see only trees, and the voice from my dream had been screaming in my ears since I had awoken. I wanted to meet people, to see new faces. But more than that, I wanted to see the Lion Boy once more. I wanted his face to be more than a memory. And I *needed* to know what else there was in the world.

So, I bid my father farewell, watching as the gate was pushed open, wishing I could dart through without anyone's notice. I still did not know how I would make it through that gate, but I was beginning to suspect I was meant to find a way.

The next day, I entered my mother's chambers, squinting in the half-light. The sun shone meekly through silk curtains, casting gray shadows upon the white walls and bedding. The rooms seemed very old and far away, with an ethereal quality like that of my mother's face. Mother sat with her back to me in a plush chair; her slender frame was draped with silk and satin in colors of deep red, like a stain of blood on a vast, pure snow. I touched her shoulder, thin as the last branch upon a dying tree. Mother did not turn.

"Mother." As I spoke, a gentle breeze blew through the open windows. Mother's hair danced, momentarily catching a shaft of sunlight and shimmering like onyx and garnet. I had always loved her dark hair. Mine was a ruddy brown that she used to tell me shone in the sun. It reminded me only of rust. But I had her eyes, the same intense green that at times made the servants nervous.

When I was small, my mother and I would play silly little games in these chambers while my sister slumbered in her bassinet. My favorite was the staring game, when we would lock our identical eyes and see who could hold the other's gaze, unblinking, for longer. Our eyes would water, and my shoulders would tremble with silent giggles, and sometimes my mother would pull a face so suddenly that I would shriek with laughter, and then shriek again to know I had lost the contest. It would wake my sister, but she never cried, only cooed with curiosity and reached for us. And my mother and I would laugh and laugh, and hold my baby sister's soft little hands.

"I am leaving, Mother," I said to her. There had been no games since my sister had died. I missed the wrinkles that used to form in the corners of my mother's eyes when she smiled.

My mother made no response.

I knelt before her. "I wish to ... to see. The world, I mean. I promised Father I wouldn't go, but ... I can't stay here any longer." I could not keep the tears from falling. I wished she would say something, anything. I wished she would grant me one small smile, that she would tell me that it was all right, that she understood.

But her eyes stared past me at nothing, at the past, or perhaps at the ghost of my sister that only she could see. She looked weary, paler even than usual, and I doubted for a moment. What if some illness befell her while I was gone?

"Please don't despair," I continued. Perhaps the pallor of her skin was a trick of my guilty mind. If I could just comfort her a little, I would have the strength to go. So I told her, "This is not goodbye. I shall return, I swear it. I just do not know when. So, farewell, I suppose. Until I do return." I kissed her cool cheek.

Then, I turned to leave, but a pressure on my arm stopped me.

"What is it, Mother?"

She was trembling, or perhaps the tears swimming in my eyes made it seem as though she were. She motioned to a small table upon which sat a gilded chest.

I had known these rooms all my life. My mother's chambers had been our sanctuary, my sister's and mine, when we were small and unburdened. They were where we had played with our dolls and with our mother's lovely clothes. The rooms smelled like her. That had been our favorite thing about them. But in all that time, I had never seen this chest before. It was like my mother had sensed that I would come here today, for this purpose, and had brought it out for me.

I lifted the chest with some difficulty and brought it to her. She rested it upon her lap as if it weighed nothing at all, and when she opened it, an inner light was set free. It flooded the room, illuminating everything in shades of silver and blue. Then it faded, and in the folds of a swath of black satin pulsed a small, carved glass vial of blue-white light. Mother lifted it tenderly and pressed it into my hands, and then her gaze slipped off me and rested longingly on the wide window.

I turned the vial over in my hands. I had never seen anything like it. It looked like something out of a fairy tale. "What is this, Mother?"

She only shook her head.

"Please, I don't understand." I tried to search her eyes, but her gaze upon the window had grown resolute. Her jaw was clenched as if she were making a great effort at something. Was she trying not to cry? I opened my mouth to say, "Don't worry, I'm sorry. I won't leave after all." But before I could speak, her eyes shot toward me once again, and there was fear in them suddenly.

"Go," she said hoarsely. "Go tonight."

"What?" I asked breathlessly.

"Go!" she cried, and fear surged through my chest. She shoved me away from her with more strength than I had imagined was left in her slight frame. "Go! Leave! Run!"

I fled her chambers, my pulse thundering in my ears, the vial clutched against my chest.

CHAPTER TWO

* * * * *

"Go tonight," my mother had said. It was the first time I had heard her voice in more than a year, and she had used it to free me from the Wall, just as I had wanted to be freed. But why had she sounded so urgent, so afraid?

I gathered my things with trembling hands, my breath hitching in my throat. My legs had tasted speed in my flight from my mother's chambers, and now they did not want to slow, but I had to wait. Mother had said "tonight," and so for night I would wait. In any case, it was only logical to wait until the servants had gone to bed and there was no one to block my path.

The hours until night were agonizing, but I waited.

I sat in a straight-backed wooden chair, uncomfortable enough to keep me from drifting to sleep. A small pack rested on my lap, filled with some clean underclothes, a skin of water I'd filched from the stables earlier, and the food I had surreptitiously slipped into the pockets of my skirts at supper. Finally, the sun set, and the servants finished their nightly chores, extinguished the candles that lit our halls, and shuffled off to bed. Everything was prepared. Finally, it was time.

I snuck Zav from the stables, and my lion and I left in the velvet night, my mother's cries and my dream's urgings mingling in my mind to spur me onward. I half feared my father would have posted guards to bar my passage, but there were none. The Wall's gate shone in the moonlight. It opened outward. I had read once in a military tome in my father's library that castle gates should open inward for better defense, but I supposed my father had been more concerned with keeping me in than with keeping anything else out. I leaned into the gate and pushed with all my strength, willing it to open, knowing it *would* open. But nothing happened.

I tried again and again. I changed my stance and dug my boots into the earth. I made a silent prayer, to whom I did not know. My eyes filled with tears, and panic started to fill my chest. Mother had said to go. The dream had said to go. It had to be this way. And yet the gate would not give way.

"Once more," I told myself. I pressed my back against the gilded metal, feeling it dig into the flesh between my shoulder blades, and then, suddenly, the pressure relented, and I stumbled backward, *outward*. Bewildered, I found Zav pressing against the gate. An opening formed gradually, large enough for a girl to slip through, almost large enough for a lion ... and then we were through. It took all my will not to shout in elation.

In the dim light from the vial hanging from my neck, I could see that the Wall on the Outside was a drab brown-gray, worn by time and grime. It was as if my world had been frozen, suspended at the day the Wall had been finished, new and shining and regal, while Outside, the world was fading to dusk.

I ran, and Zav followed, leaving puddles of moonlight behind us as we entered into the swirling mists of the forest. I did not slow my steps until the trees grew thick around us. Upon my breast, the gentle light of my mother's vial pulsed in time with my heartbeat, and Zav's paws padded softly over the bracken-covered earth. We slowed our pace and our breathing and drifted through the tall trees, directionless. When I looked back, I saw nothing but trees.

I had considered leaving a letter for my father but decided against it. There was nothing I could say on parchment that my departure did not say for me. And perhaps my mother had found her voice again for good, I allowed myself to hope. Perhaps *she* would tell my father, and it would be all right that I was gone, for she had urged me to go.

But as I walked on in the darkness, my feet splashing through pools of white moonlight that spilled through gaps in the trees, my hands shaking, I realized the enormity of breaking my promise to him. I had sworn never to set foot outside the Wall, and I had gone, quite alone, out into the world my father had always feared so. And something told me there would be little my mother could say—even if she did manage to speak—that would assuage his worry. I drew my velvet cloak close around my body and pulled the hood over my head, but it only felt like more darkness, so I took the cloak off and laid it over Zav's back. I shivered in my thin dress but felt emboldened by my mother's light, foreign to me though it was.

Zav and I walked into the sunrise. Our feet found it first, and we gleamed like moon and sun as we entered into its light, which grew through the trees and bushes. I watched it rise above the treetops and pour down upon us. I was very tired. The sun crept along to shine upon the back of my head, and Zav was alive with golden fire.

We stopped at a fallen tree, thicker than three of the birch trees near the Wall bound together. There, the land sighed a great sigh and then fell, and Zav and I climbed down into the basin below the land's rise. We lay in the soft grass, sheltered by the slope of the land on three sides, and there we slept through the day until the sun was setting at our feet.

I dined on food pilfered from the kitchens within the Wall, and Zav caught a hare, which he ate happily, and we stayed the night in the haven of the sighing land. The night noises did not trouble me, for Zav was at my side.

I awoke the next morning to a sound like the beating of a hundred wings. Sitting up with a jolt, I scanned the ground, the skies, the trees, but all I saw was one solitary raven.

"Was that you?" I asked it, trying to slow my racing heart.

The raven clicked its beak, and for a moment, I felt silly for being so startled by one bird. But then it bobbed its head at me, hopped to a lower tree branch, and croaked, "Death."

My chest tightened. Birds did not speak. Birds could not speak. Or could they? I had only seen ravens in the pages of books.

"Death," it said again.

"Zav!" I cried. Zav stirred, making a deep sound in the back of his throat. He caught sight of the raven and growled hungrily.

"Death." The bird stared at us, its eyes too knowing. I fought the urge to flee. But then Zav roared in warning, and the raven flew off in a flurry of black feathers. The sound of its wings lingered long after it was gone.

I put my hand on Zav's side. "We need to go," I said, my voice low. We headed up the gentle slope, back towards the trees, slowly at first. But as we moved, I felt an urgency that I could not place. I quickened my pace, and Zav matched me. I could feel something on the back of my neck, something icy, like a winter wind had crept its way into the forest. I turned back for only a moment, but that moment was filled with a darkness thicker than that of the night, with satin creases and velvet folds, and it seemed ... alive.

It had been morning just moments before, yet the sky had grown so dark I could barely make out the shapes of the trees and brush. "What *is* that?"

"Run!" It was the raven. It flew overhead, its midnight-purple underbelly mirroring the oncoming darkness. It let out a sound like a laugh, but it was mirthless and nearly as cold as the wind that now bit at me.

Zav and I complied. Swiftly, he shouldered me onto his broad back, and I lay flat against him as he loped through the forest. We flew through the trees, the raven above us, cackling in a way that no creature should have been able to laugh. The forest behind us was sucked into blackness and the trees gave way as something much darker flooded through them. Zav ran so quickly that the world was a blur. My hand slipped. The familiar sensation of falling overtook me.

* ✳ ✳ ✳ *

CHAPTER THREE

* ✳ ✳ ✳ *

I sat up with a great deal of effort. My head ached, and I was still shivering.

"Zav!" I stood, but fell again as a rush of pain swayed me. I tried again to stand, moving slowly until I was rocking on unsteady legs. "Zav!" I called again. I turned, panicked, but Zav's rumbling growl eased my fears. He padded up to me, and I leaned against his side and looked around at the forest. There was nothing strange about it. It was just a midmorning forest rustling in the easy wind.

There was no sign of the raven.

I sighed in relief. "That was awful," I whispered.

"What was?"

I gasped and whirled to face the questioner.

"Did that mean old hag give you a fright?" asked the child before me. She had sandy skin and sandy hair and a smiling face. She was carrying two pails of water on a staff across her back. "She'll do no real harm—oh, but you're bleeding! The wretch, she'll not find any sympathy from me, not now at any rate. Mum will fix you up—she fixes everyone. Will the lion bite?"

"I'm sorry?"

"'E won't bite me, will 'e? Mum may fix, but it should still hurt like the god knows what, I'd suspect."

"I'm sorry, the what?"

The child giggled and took my hand. "Come on then," she said, and I found myself walking with her up a hill toward a small cottage, the water upon Zav's able shoulders.

We arrived hand in hand at a little home with a smoking chimney and rows of herbs and flowers standing sentinel along a stone path.

"Hallo!" the child at my side called out.

"Annie, are you back with the water?" A handsome, pregnant woman stepped out of the cottage, smiling, her hands at her back. "Ah, a lion! And a noble-looking one at that. I haven't seen one of his kind around here since I was a girl." She bobbed her head in my direction. "Now then, child, what's your name?"

"Julia," I lied.

"Lady Julia, I suspect," replied the pregnant woman.

"Mum, the crone tricked Julia in the woods. That's how she knocked her head."

I put my hand to my forehead, and my fingers came away bloody. I hadn't even realized I was bleeding.

"Yes, yes, Annie. Go and fetch a rag. Here then, Lady Julia, come and sit."

I took the stool the woman offered me beside the herb garden, and Zav settled in beside me. Annie's mother—Sophie, she told me to call her—cleaned the cut on my forehead and gave me bread and cheese to eat, smiling all the while. She and Annie were the first people I had spoken to in years, aside from my parents and the aging servants at the Wall, who had always kept their distance from me.

I no longer knew how to talk to new people. Luckily, Annie did enough talking for the both of us.

The crone, Annie told me in a low voice, as if telling a particularly thrilling secret, had lived in these woods for eighteen years, though none had ever seen her. She occasionally "threw fits," in Annie's words, kicking up storms, or tainting a well, or causing a crop to fail, and if one wandered too deep into the forest—"In the direction *you* came from, in fact," Annie added with a hushed sort of awe—the crone would turn them around until they were hopelessly lost. People would wander for hours, sometimes even days, before finding themselves back on the outskirts of the woods.

"It's gotten worse of late," Annie concluded. "Hasn't it, Mum?"

Her mother chuckled. "Pay her no mind, Lady Julia. All the commoners around these parts have ghost stories about the forest. But really the paths are just overgrown and treacherous, so folk don't venture in very often. And no one has ever seen any crone. Annie just likes to give herself a good scare."

I furrowed my brow. I had been alive for eighteen years. The Wall had stood for eighteen years. And we *had* seen far fewer travelers passing through than there had been when I was a girl. Could it be that something really was keeping them away? I had certainly experienced something frightful in the forest, something that had driven me to its outskirts ... I shook my head. No. There was nothing sinister in the forest—in *my* forest. I had lived at its heart my whole life. Surely I would know if some dark power had resided just outside the Wall that entire time.

I considered moving on after Sophie had tended to my forehead, but she insisted I stay. "Just for today," she assured me. "I'd like to watch over you just a little while."

No one had watched over me in so long.

I consented. We spent the day kneading dough and picking vegetables, and as night fell, Sophie offered me a straw mat by the stove to sleep upon. She brought me warm milk to drink before I fell asleep. She reminded me of my mother when she smiled, though I hadn't seen my mother smile in years.

I missed her smile. She had seemed frailer by the day these past years, but she was not always so. Not long after my sister's birth, I had become terribly ill. I was feverish, sweating and shivering and vomiting for days. My parents were distraught, the servants were afraid, and once, deep in the night, when they thought I was asleep, the cook, bringing hot water to my bedside, had whispered to the maid, "I reckon she'll pass on, the poor lamb, don't you?"

"She most certainly will not," my mother had said, in the coldest tones I had ever heard her use. The servants had not known she was there in the shadows beside me, any more than they had known I was awake. "My daughter has a strength you could not know. She will recover," my mother continued. "And if you've nothing hopeful to say, you had best hold your tongues."

I remembered how my heart swelled when my mother called me strong. For days, she sat by my side, and I felt lucky to have her all to myself. Later, my mother would praise me for my courage, reminding me that my only complaint during my illness was that I wasn't allowed to play with my infant sister.

Julia. That was my sister's name. That was the name I had given to this kind family in place of my own. Although they had welcomed me, I did not want to be too trusting. In the storybooks, if a witch knew your name, she could steal your face, and I quite preferred my face attached to the front of my head. So I lied. What did they need with my true name anyway?

The next morning dawned with the smell of baked bread and herbs and a hint of horse manure, and I was certain I smelled of it all as well. Half of me wanted to stay with Annie and her mother longer, to live simply and to work hard, but I needed to move on. So I bade them farewell and continued along my way, riding on Zav's back.

Using the directions Annie's mother had given me, I found the main road after only a few hours and followed it northeast through rows of strangely uniform trees to a place unlike any I had ever heard of or imagined. We had reached a city. Ivory buildings with tall towers and golden pinnacles draped with vibrant banners greeted us as we walked into the city. I marveled at the open markets—the bazaars and the kiosks and the merchants all milling about, calling out their various wares. What thrilled me most, however, was that the city had no wall. It was open to the trees and the road.

I worried that Zav would be out of place, but the streets were filled with exotic creatures; some were in cages, some were bound by silver chains, but some simply roamed, following a whim or a master, or a whiff of food from somewhere deep in the market. Zav let out a soft whimper as we neared a tiny lion cub in a golden cage. I traced the bars with my fingers until I noticed an old merchant scowling at me.

"If you ain't buyin' him, you've no call fer touchin'."

"I beg your pardon. It's just ... what will happen to him?"

"Well, if ye get along yer way, maybe I'll be able to sell him to some'ne respectable like, get a pretty penny for him."

"That seems awfully cruel," I murmured.

The merchant grinned in a way I did not care for. "And how do ye think ye got yer beast there, eh?"

I stared at him, hurt, and then turned away, wondering if the Lion Boy could really have been so heartless. To take a creature as noble as Zav and sell him to the highest bidder seemed a terrible thing to do. I scanned the crowd but did not see the Lion Boy. I hadn't truly expected him to be there, but I did not know where to even begin my search.

I passed a silk merchant selling fabrics in colors too rich to be real, a young boy selling flowers and herbs, a perfumer whose stall smelled like muddled dreams. There were rugs and bangles and baskets and pottery and all sorts of weaponry and clothing, and all manner of customers eating and drinking and spending small fortunes left and right. It was all so bustling and opulent.

But the farther into the city Zav and I roamed, the less beautiful it became. The narrow walkways between the white buildings were shrouded in shadow, doors were barred with wooden planks, and thick, dark awnings blocked out the sun. I longed for the chaos of the market, the light of day, and the comforting chatter of the crowd, but I wasn't sure I remembered the way back.

"What have we here?"

I turned sharply, aware of the fear in my eyes as I looked up at the man who had spoken. I could smell him—pungent, sharp, and sour. I moved closer to Zav.

"A lost little bird," the man continued. He smiled through rotten teeth and, looking past me, asked, "Isn't that right?"

I looked over my shoulder. Another, equally revolting man stood behind me, grinning menacingly.

"What do you want?"

"We want the lion," said a familiar, rasping voice. I turned to see the old man from the market, standing with his arms crossed. He nodded to the man closer to me, who grabbed me tightly around the middle, pinning my arms to my sides.

"No!" I shrieked. "No! Let me go!"

Zav roared, but before he could pounce, two more men had thrown a net over him, and he began to moan and growl. The old merchant stood before me. He brushed my hair from my face and I began to cry.

"She could make a pretty penny as well," he mused.

"No!" I cried. "You can't! Please, let me go. *Please!*" I struggled against the man at my back, but he held me fast, and he squeezed so hard I could barely breathe.

The merchant laughed. "Good work, lads." He turned away, and I knew he meant for them to do with me as they liked.

I thrashed as hard as I could as the men closed in on me. I was half-blind with terror. My breath hitched in my throat, and I thought I might faint, but knew if I did, my fate was sealed. One man stepped forward and leaned in to taunt me, his eyes so close to mine they blurred in my vision.

Then, suddenly, those eyes were wide with pain and surprise, and the man fell forward into me, and I screamed. Men were shouting, Zav was roaring, and a sound like a harp string twanged through the air thrice more, and a man dropped from the sky onto the man behind me, and I was rolling on the cobblestones. I landed face to face with a dead man. I saw that the one who had held me lay beside him, motionless, and the merchant was dead as well, farther off toward the mouth of the alley. All shot through with arrows.

A man dressed in leathers with a bow and quiver upon his back straightened from where he had knelt over the man who had held me.

I crawled to Zav, wrestled the net off him, then threw my arms around his neck and buried my face in his mane. I wanted to stay like that forever, safe beside my lion. But I also knew that my savior could be dangerous as well. I moved to Zav's haunches, ready to spur him into action should this man prove as sinister as the others.

"Are you all right?"

"I'm fine, thank you," I replied, my voice shaking.

The man with the bow furrowed a handsome brow. "Let me help you."

"No, thank you," I said stiffly, and trembling, brought myself to my feet. Zav rose with me.

The man took a step toward me, and I tensed. He seemed to sense my hesitance. He stopped not far from Zav's muzzle, and despite my fear, I noticed that Zav's hackles had lowered, his body relaxed. He did not seem to fear this stranger.

The man was much taller than I was and had darker skin. He brushed wavy, deep brown locks out of his face and looked at me with concern upon his striking features.

"What were you doing down here, anyway? It's dangerous, you know."

"Really? Is it?" I asked, forcing the sarcasm into my voice. My cheeks burned.

He furrowed his brow again. "What's your name?"

"Lady Julia."

He raised an eyebrow.

"What?" I asked.

He chuckled. "'Lady' is it?"

"Yes," I said tersely. Did he think me a liar or was he toying with me? "And what is your name?" I asked. "I assume it isn't *Lord*." I had met a few lords, when they had visited the Wall. All of them had dressed in lush fabrics, not the rough linens and leathers this young man wore. And none of them had seemed to make a habit of leaping from balconies whilst firing arrows.

He chuckled again. "No. It is Eytan, of Bahir."

"Bahir!" My irritation was forgotten in my excitement. The Great City of Bahir was the capital of Midbar, clear across the Calder Sea. I had read of it often in my father's books. Its people called it the land of milk and honey and considered it a blessed oasis amidst the desert that surrounded it. As a child, I had thought they meant the title literally, that the very sand there tasted of honey, and that the desert springs flowed with sweet milk instead of water.

"How did you get here?"

"Aboard a ship," Eytan said, as if that should have been obvious.

"All the way from Midbar? How long did it take?"

"A month or so—don't you know that?"

"How should I know how long it takes to cross the Calder Sea?"

"You're a lady," he said simply. "You mean to tell me you've never sailed the Calder?"

I shook my head and started to speak, but the sound of voices from somewhere close by stopped me. Eytan looked around and held a hand out to me.

"We should go. Come on."

I hesitated, but Zav had already moved to Eytan of Bahir's side, seemingly perfectly happy to follow this stranger. So I took his outstretched hand, startled that it felt so easy. I had never held someone's hand before, other than my mother's. Eytan's was larger, rougher, warmer. I tried to ignore the sensation.

Zav loped at my side as Eytan led us swiftly down a side street, then another and another, until we were back in the busy market, where we blended easily into the crowd.

* * * * *

CHAPTER FOUR

* * * * *

Dusk had fallen, and Eytan thought it wise to stay off the streets for the night since the death of several merchants—criminals though they had turned out to be—was sure to raise suspicion. He found us two rooms at an inn outside of town, which he offered to pay for, much to my dismay. I had some coin, but not enough to last terribly long. It was just one more thing that had not occurred to me upon leaving the Wall, and I was so humiliated by the oversight that I nearly turned around and returned home then and there. But I had come this far. I accepted Eytan's offer. After we had settled Zav in the stables beside some very distraught horses, we ate our evening meal in the inn's common room. As I picked at my food, I stared at Eytan intently.

"What are you looking at?" he asked.

"Just because you saved my life does not mean I trust you," I told him.

He nodded. "No, you don't seem that sort."

"You killed those men."

"They were going to hurt you."

My stomach turned, and I found I was no longer hungry. "Yes," I said, "I know." I brushed some grime from my dress, realizing for the first time just how wretched the world could be. "Then, you don't feel guilty?"

He gave me a puzzled look. "They were going to hurt you," he said again, as if that explained everything. "Anyway, the law won't trouble me for it. Far worse happens in those back alleys of the city."

I shuddered to think what worse there could be.

"What are you doing wandering about alone anyway?" he asked.

"I'm not alone. Zav is with me."

He chuckled and took a sip of ale. "That isn't quite what I meant."

"I am looking for someone," I said simply.

"A friend?"

"Not exactly. A boy I knew once. Zav was a gift from him. I suppose I want to thank him ... for his generosity." In truth, I had no idea what I would say to the Lion Boy if I ever found him. I was not even sure why I was looking for him.

"What was his name?" Eytan asked.

"I ... I don't know." I could feel my cheeks growing hot at the admission.

"What *do* you know?"

I took a large bite of the meat pie in front of me to allow myself time to think. "Well," I said after I had swallowed, "he looked Midbari, and he was about my age—maybe a bit older. He must have been a noble of some means, to gift me with Zav. And he thought I would like pink."

"Did you?"

"No."

He frowned. "You don't exactly have much to go on. Midbar is a large realm."

"That much I am aware of."

Eytan raised an eyebrow. "Well, do you want me to take you there, or not?"

I opened and closed my mouth a few times in what I was sure was a stunning impression of a gasping fish.

"Why, no!" I finally managed.

"*No?*"

"No! I most certainly do *not* want you to take me there. I have yet to decide if I even trust you. Do you offer this sort of thing often? *Really!* Taking girls off across the sea. Just what are you about?"

A strange look passed over Eytan's face, and he stared into the fire behind me. "I don't," he said simply.

"What?"

"I don't offer this sort of thing often. I only thought I'd help. Apparently, you would rather be alone, so I'll go." He stood and headed toward the door. I watched him go somewhat helplessly, wondering if I would always make a mess of things in the Outside.

"Wait!" I finally called after him. My foolish mouth ...

I rushed out the door of the inn just in time to see Eytan's figure receding into the darkness.

"Wait!" I shouted. I chased him into the night. He was walking so quickly that I could barely keep pace.

"Please, wait! I'm sorry, I was only trying ... I did not mean ... I—" I grabbed Eytan's elbow to stop him but succeeded in stumbling into him instead. He caught me easily, chuckling a little.

I straightened and pulled free of him. I could feel my cheeks growing red again, and I scowled, more out of embarrassment than anger.

"We shall make an agreement," I declared.

"We shall?"

I set my hands on my hips. "You may *help* me find my way to Midbar, but I will repay you."

"How generous of you. And how do you intend to repay me?"

"Well, my ... my father has some wealth. I am sure he would ... well ..."

"Do you have no money of your own?" Eytan asked.

"Well, only a bit. I suppose I just assumed ..." I don't know what I had assumed, in truth. In my urgency and my fear at my mother's words, I had failed to think through my flight at all. I suppose I thought perhaps I could find some work somewhere, but that too seemed foolish now that I was out in the world. What skills did I have, anyway? There did not seem to be much need in the Outside for my extensive knowledge of fairy tales or my mediocre ability to embroider. Perhaps I could travel to the deserts of Midbar and earn my keep as a lion tamer. I had taught Zav some impressive tricks, after all.

Eytan laughed again, maybe at my foolishness, maybe at my brooding face as I reflected on my predicament. "All right. It is not money that I desire in any case. But there is something you can do for me."

Narrowing my eyes, I said, "What's that?"

"You can let me show you things."

I backed away. "What sorts of things?" I asked dubiously.

"Oh," Eytan shrugged, following me, "you know—the world. I have business in a few places in these parts before I return to Midbar. I could show you things along the way. Cities and towns. The great stallions of the Northern Mountains, the Aelfin Forests, the temples of the Gaea, the outlaws of Firth. Don't you want to see all that?"

"There *are* stallions!" I exclaimed.

"Sorry?"

"In the mountains of the North. There really are stallions up there?"

He began to walk back towards the inn, and I fell into step beside him. "Folk say they are made from the snowdrifts."

I knew I had seen them! My heart began to swell with excitement. "What else?" I asked. "What else can we see?"

"Well, there are the swordsmiths of Oro, the knights of Saberhold. I could take you to see the weaver women of the Halli Islands, we could see whales swimming in the Azurae Sea, or we could go to the Singing Mountains of the West and see the stars shine over the whole of the land." He shrugged again, like it made little difference to him.

"The world has all of that?"

"And that is only here in Gaerwn. I could show you such wonderful things in Midbar."

A thousand golden adventures flashed before my eyes. I beamed. "And we could really see all of it?" I asked.

We were outside our quarters now, and he opened the door to his rooms. "Well, we could. But I understand you are probably anxious to find your friend, so I can put my business on hold. We should find the nearest port and make our way to Midbar. No time to prattle about." And with that, he slipped inside and shut the door behind him.

I stood in the hall, dumbfounded. "But, the Lion Boy could be anywhere!" I called desperately through the door. And I *so* wanted to see the stallions of the North. But he made no response, so I returned to my room, wondering if I should have left the Wall in the first place.

I did not sleep well. My mattress was stiff and moldering, and the walls creaked all through the night. I awoke many times, worrying over Zav, and I had nightmares about the Wall. It crumbled, it burned, it awoke and screamed in pain. My father screamed too.

I awoke in the dark with that scream echoing in my ears, and I suddenly felt that I had made a terrible mistake. I had left in the night, left my mother alone in that house, haunted by the painful memories that I had been selfish enough to shrug off. She had told me to run, but she had been ill for a long, long while. How could I have left her in such a state? And my father ... he would return home and find me gone, find my mother sicker than ever, find himself alone.

How could I be so selfish?

A draft through the inn's thin walls seized upon my bare skin, and I could swear I felt that man's hands clamp onto me again—the man from the market. I may not have known much of the world, but I knew what those men would have done to me had Eytan not appeared. And what would they have done to Zav? Sold him? Turned him into some pack mule? Killed him and skinned him for his pelt? Those thoughts horrified me almost more than the thoughts of what would have become of me. I pulled my knees up to my chest. Suddenly, I could not stop trembling, but it had little to do with the cold.

And what of Eytan? Yes, he had saved me, and yes, Zav seemed to trust him. But Zav knew little more of the world than I did. And Eytan *had* killed five men. He had done it to save me, but did that make it right? It had not even seemed to give him pause to do such a thing.

"I have to go home," I whispered into the night.

* * *

It seemed that stealing away in the night was the one thing I was good for. I packed my meager belongings, scrawled a quick note to Eytan and slipped it under his door, and then I was gone. Zav rumbled inquisitively as I slipped into the stables, but he followed me willingly, although I thought I saw him steal a longing glance back at the inn where Eytan slept, ignorant to our flight.

"I'm sorry, Zav," I told him, "but we can't stay here. Mother needs us." Saying the words aloud steeled my resolve, and we set off into the night, back down the road to our forest, back to where my mother awaited me.

* * * * *

CHAPTER FIVE

* * * * *

We walked through the night once more, but I was more afraid than I had been on my first journey into the world. I now knew what dangers the Outside held. The Wall may have been suffocating, but at least it was safe.

We followed the main road to the southwest, back towards Annie's cottage. Perhaps I could stop there and offer them my thanks for their hospitality. But what had I to offer them, really? Fool that I was, I still had almost no coin to my name. A small part of me had considered stealing a few silvers from Eytan—I would have my father send him reimbursement once I was safely home, I reasoned. But that seemed a cold thing to do to a man who had been so kind to me, a man who had killed for me. Just because the world was cold did not mean I had to be.

My feet slowed and I looked to the east. Surely it should be sunrise by now, but I saw only a faint haze on the horizon. The air was heavy, humid. It had an odd taste to it, as if a storm was on its way. When I turned back to look at the road, I blinked in surprise. The road had ... ended. Before us was the forest, appearing where it should not yet have appeared, a tangle of gnarled trees and bushes with thorns as sharp as steel.

"Did we come this way before?" I whispered to Zav.

We must have taken a wrong turning, I thought. But how had I failed to notice such a cruel wall of trees lurking right in front of us? Perhaps it had been lost in the mists, for fog was indeed rolling in. Zav made an uncertain sound.

"Maybe we should turn back." I tried to keep the quaver out of my voice. I pressed closer to Zav and steered him around. The main road stretched out before us, but there was something different about it. It was like a dark tunnel, walled with trees that stood like sentries. Those trees looked grayer somehow than they had before ...

I looked over my shoulder again, but the landscape seemed to slide out of my vision, painted in dark watercolors that bled off the corners of their canvas. My breathing came quicker. I had lost all sense of direction. Home was to the south, Eytan to the north, but which way was which, I could not have said. It was then that the rain began.

I had never felt such icy rain. Fat raindrops so cold they almost burned pounded down on us, and Zav began to wail. I turned a circle, but all I could see was the main road lined with those sinister trees on one side, a wall of thorns and old oaks on the other, and a roiling fog pressing in from every direction.

I swallowed my fear as best I could. We could not stay where we were. "Zav!" I shouted over the downpour. "Follow me!"

I swept my cloak off my shoulders and over Zav's haunches, then launched myself into the twisted, tangled trees, shielding my face from the razor thorns. We pushed deeper into the forest, both of us crying out in pain as the thorns tore at us, but at least the trees' canopy was too thick for the rain to penetrate much. I found a place where the thorn bushes' boughs were bent in a low arc, forming what looked like a massive, upturned nest. For a brief moment, I imagined some monstrous bird returning to this nest and devouring Zav and myself whole. But it was the best shelter we had available to us, and I did not like the look of this part of the forest.

We hunched down and inched into the nest, careful not to touch its thorny sides. I pulled my cloak off of Zav and checked him for cuts. He had a few shallow scratches, but none that seemed to be causing him too much pain. The sleeves of my dress had been cut to ribbons, and my skin stung and smarted.

Blood trickled down my arms, but there was nothing I could do about that now. I wrapped the cloak back around me to stanch the flow of blood and stroked Zav, to calm myself as much as him.

"We'll wait out the rain here," I told him. I could still hear it drumming away beyond the trees, and far above us as well.

And though I was terrified and soaked through, freezing and in pain, I found I was suddenly so weary that I could do nothing but curl up against Zav and sleep.

I dreamed.

I was back within the Wall, but something was different. It seemed far older. The glistening white of its inner surfaces had faded to gray, whithered vines grew up its length, and bits of stone had chipped away, leaving it pockmarked. It looked like a pale moon in a clouded sky. In my dream, I knew not to touch the surface of the stone, for it held secrets that would burn my very heart.

Someone was singing. The wind picked up the thin strains of music and carried them off into the forest. I knew I had to find the source of the tune. I knew many things in dreams.

I crossed the courtyard, and the grass crumbled and turned to ash beneath my feet. This did not alarm me; some things are normal in dreams that in reality seem strange. Of course, the grass would not grow here. Nothing could grow within the Wall. Nothing could change. It seemed perfectly reasonable, too, that the great doors of my family home were flung open before me, creaking in the wind. Why close doors when there is a wall to protect you? I was meant to go through those doors. That was where the music emanated from. I could taste its melody on my tongue, bittersweet like a tincture, or like poison.

Inside, the house was ... wrong. There was no furniture, no paintings or tapestries. Even the chandelier that should have hung above the foyer was missing, and I could swear I heard the echoes of metal crashing and crystal shattering throughout the hall. Only the bones of the house remained, picked clean by time or bandits or maybe by my absence. And clean it was. The walls, the floors, the railings were well-polished. There was not a cobweb to be found, nor a single speck of dust upon a single surface. It was a clean thing, yes, but a dead thing—dead in a way that made me want to turn and flee, made me want to clutch my head and collapse and scream in madness.

The melody grew louder.

I ascended the stairs and knew immediately from where the music was originating. It was obvious, dream or no. It was inevitable. I made my way to my mother's chambers.

Just as in the rest of the house, her rooms were devoid of decoration or furnishings, save her rocking chair, and that was where she sat, facing curtainless windows, singing a song in a tongue I did not recognize, not even in dreams. Her beautiful hair spilled down her back. Pale hands gripped the arms of the chair. The chair rocked steadily, forth and back, forth and back. It creaked with each motion. Her voice warbled with each note.

I reached out to her, but my dream knowledge stayed my hand. If touching the Wall would burn me in this place, touching my mother would turn me straight to ash, until I blew out the window, on the wind with her song, and mingled with the ash that was the grass of the courtyard, and there I would remain. I tried to speak, but my mouth was full of ash already. I could not stay here much longer.

I knew somehow that looking upon my mother's face in this place would break me, but I also knew I had to look. I needed to look the same way I had needed to leave the Wall. Willful blindness would trap me just as surely as the dangers of this dream world could. And so I walked around the rocking chair, giving it a wide berth, until I stood facing my mother.

Her cheeks were sunken in, her skin was shriveled, her mouth hung open, gaping black, filled with maggots. I stared. Dead eyes stared back at me.

I awoke sobbing.

I heaved deep breaths and coughed, expecting ash to spew out of my mouth, or maggots. I retched into the grass. I scrubbed at my face with my hands, half expecting my skin to slough off, like it would off some dead thing, but my hands came away touched only by the salt of my tears.

Zav was standing, moaning at me, tugging at my cloak with his teeth. I looked around us. It was morning. We were in a clearing, surrounded by the sparse trees that marked the outer boundaries of the forest. The frightful bird's nest from the night before was merely a low thicket. There were no brambles, no thorns in sight. I could see the main road stretching out before us. Had it *all* been a dream?

Zav's tugging at my cloak and the fear that remained coiled in my stomach told me that some of it, at least, had been real. He was pulling me toward the main road, away from the forest and the Wall, back toward Eytan. I knew he was right. My dream had been telling me something, warning me of something. I could not return to the Wall. Besides, there was nothing left for me there now.

I hoped that Eytan had not risen yet and found me gone. Something told me I hoped in vain, though. He struck me as an early riser. I felt guilty for abandoning him, but that guilt was overwhelmed by my desperation to return to him, to have someone at my side who could tell me it would be all right. I had known him only a day, but I already missed his presence. I prayed he had not already left the inn.

The morning had brought with it the chill of autumn, and the breeze stung my exposed arms. I looked down and saw that the sleeves of my dress, and the skin underneath, were in tatters. The thorns, then, had not been a dream. A wave of panic rose in me, and I tried my best to quell it. There had to be some explanation. Zav and I had fled into the thorns to escape a cruel storm. Perhaps we had wandered farther than I had realized, and by the time we came to the thicket, we had entered a friendlier part of the forest. Perhaps I had not realized how much of the woods we had traversed, given the mist and the rain and my distress.

A quiet voice within me that I did not wish to heed told me this was not the case.

When I saw Eytan, all thoughts of dark forests and dark dreams dissipated. He was sitting beneath a willow tree outside the inn, his pack, his bow, and his quiver at his side. He looked like he was waiting for someone. When he saw me, his face broke into a smile. He was waiting for me.

"I was hoping you'd come back," he called.

My heart swelled and I ran to him, standing on the tips of my toes to fling my arms around his neck. I wanted to laugh and cry all at once. I supposed I had needed the comfort of a warm embrace. Eytan returned the embrace, slowly at first. As his arms wrapped securely around my waist, I finally felt safe again.

"Julia!" he said, pulling away from me and holding my wrists. "What happened to your arms?"

* * * *

CHAPTER SIX
* * * *

Eytan paid again for a room at the inn—just one room this time, which caused the innkeep to raise an eyebrow. He requested hot water, sat me down on the room's straw mattress, and pulled a small, stout blade from his boot.

I leaned back, narrowing my eyes. "Just what do you think you're doing?"

He chuckled. "I'm going to cut your sleeves away. So I can clean your wounds."

"But I'll be exposed."

Raising his eyebrows, he replied, "You're exposed now."

I could not argue with that. I let him cut the ribbons of fabric away, leaving my arms completely bare. I blushed.

He winced. "These scratches are deep."

"There were thorns ..."

A knock at the door signaled that the hot water had arrived. Eytan retrieved it, took a cloth, and began dabbing at my wounds.

"Where did you go?" he asked gently.

"I ... I tried to go back home." I could feel the tears rolling down my cheeks, but I was too weary to wipe them away. "I felt I had abandoned my mother."

He was watching me carefully, his deep brown eyes gentle and filled with worry.

"But I ... there was ... I got lost. And then I dreamed ..." I shook my head.

"You can tell me." His voice was so soft it nearly broke my heart.

But I was not ready to speak what I knew to be true. Instead, I shook my head again, sniffled, and forced a smile. "It's nothing. I'm weary, that's all."

I could tell he knew there was more to it than that, but mercifully, he did not press me. Instead, he smiled gently and finished cleaning my wounds in silence. From his pack, he drew an extra tunic and handed it to me. "You can wear this under your dress," he said. "To cover your arms."

"Thank you."

"Why don't I let you rest here for a few hours? I can wake you for supper if you'd like."

I nodded, clutching the tunic tightly in my hands. It smelled like him. It was a pleasant smell. "I'd like that," I replied.

I met Eytan downstairs that evening, and we shared a light supper. I could not help watching him as he ate.

Finally, he sighed and replaced his spoon in his stew. "May I help you?"

I smiled. I could tell he was jesting to cheer me. I played with my stew. "Do you think I am going about this wrong?" I asked at length.

"You seem to have a fair handle on the use of a spoon," he replied.

"What? Oh, no, not my supper!" I flushed. Now he thought me so dim that I could not even eat properly.

Eytan chuckled. "I was joking."

I sighed. I was grateful to him for all he had done, but I was finding him a bit difficult. "I meant my quest. I am never going to find the Lion Boy."

"Probably not."

"What have I done?" I said it more to myself than to him, but he looked at me gently.

"I could take you home if that is what you want. It is not too late. And I have ... more experience navigating than you do."

I did not know what I wanted. I did not know what home was. Could the

Wall be home? It had never felt that way to me. It had seemed more of a prison, and my mother and father had seemed prisoners as much as I was. But home ... I had never been there.

"My mother is dead," I whispered.

Eytan made no response. His warm eyes searched mine, and he waited for me to speak.

"It happened last night," I continued. "I felt her go. I ... I saw it in a dream. While I was in the forest." I drew the vial she had given me from beneath the collar of my dress. I had noticed something different about it when I had disrobed to don Eytan's tunic. "I don't know how. But the light has gone out. She is gone."

I felt Eytan's hand upon mine, rough and warm, protecting me. "I am sorry."

I nodded. I wanted to cry, but I could not. It was all so distant, so surreal. So I smiled grimly.

"I do not want to go home," I said. "I want to see the stallions of the North. Will you take me?"

I cried that night. Eytan, Zav, and I had settled along the roadside because the inn had begun to feel oppressive to me. I worried irrationally that the thorns from the forest would creep out towards it and envelope us in our sleep. Somehow, moving further away from that forest felt safer. Still, the fire Eytan built up stung my eyes and the ground was hard and unforgiving and the chill night air seemed to reach right to my bones. When the tears began, I turned my face away, but he saw. He knew.

"Julia."

I looked at him and could not have predicted what I said next. "Have you ever been in love?" I asked.

He sat silent for a moment and then said, "No. I thought I was, years ago. But I was just a boy. And we were not acquainted. That is, I knew her well, but she ... she did not know me." He smiled unconvincingly.

I did not press him.

* * *

I knew, of course, that traveling with a veritable stranger was unwise at best, even if he *had* saved my life. But my mother had bid me leave the Wall, and only days after I had gone, she had died. And I somehow *knew*. That had to mean something. I thought about Annie's ominous remarks about a witch in the forest, about how the trouble this witch caused had grown more frequent of late, about how folk said it had been eighteen years since all of it had started. And I thought of my mother's wide, fearful eyes when she told me to flee.

Perhaps there *was* a witch in the forest. Perhaps the Wall was meant to keep her out, and she had only grown more powerful in her years of waiting for her chance to strike. I pictured a terrible old hag crouching in a cave somewhere, practicing her evil spells. Maybe my mother had sensed her power growing, and that was why she had told me to leave. Why a witch would want to harm my mother was beyond me, but the more I imagined it, the sharper the image became. Yes, the witch had seen her opening, with my father and me both gone, and had descended upon our home and killed my mother.

That must have been it. She must have chased me out of the woods to ensure that I would not return and disturb her vile plans. And when I *had* tried to return, she attacked me. So now I could not go back. For I could picture the witch haunting the halls of my childhood home, laying claim to everything that had once been my mother's, my father's, mine.

I shook my head and tried to dispel the silly horror story I had concocted. I was making excuses, I told myself. I wanted to see the world; I did not want to take responsibility for leaving the Wall. There was no witch. My mother had been ill for several years. I felt her pass because I was a part of her, and she a part of me. There was no evil magic in that. But still, the desperation in her voice when she had told me to leave ... That had not seemed like illness, or like madness.

Witch or no witch, the thought of returning to the Wall now terrified me.

It took more than a week to reach the Northern Mountains. They had once had a name in the old language, but now it was long dead, swept away by years of snow.

It made me sad to think that they were now nameless, but I did not spend much time on musings. I was too busy being cold. Zav did not seem to mind the cold, nor did Eytan. I, on the other hand, was freezing. Snow leaked through my laced boots and wool stockings, and drafts snaked into the folds of my velvet cloak. Yet, somehow, Eytan's light leather garb kept him from giving the slightest shiver.

"Aren't you cold?" I asked, shouting over the wind.

"I suppose I'm used to it."

I raised an eyebrow. "Your home is a desert."

Eytan simply laughed, and we walked a while longer. I peered at the banks of snow that surrounded us, feeling swallowed by the mountains.

"I don't see the horses."

He stood behind me and put a hand on my shoulder. Pointing up at a high ridge, he said, "There."

I squinted against sunlight that seemed far brighter and far purer than any I had known before, and I searched the snow for some sign of movement. Suddenly, I saw them. Glistening forms that seemed composed entirely of snow reared up, pure white horses prancing on the mountainside. My breath caught in my throat.

"They are beautiful!"

Eytan beamed. "I thought you would like them."

I had never known anyone to smile as much as he did. But then, I had not known many people in my life.

"What are they?"

"Some say they are the spirits of horses who died in the service of their riders, others claim them an enchantment cast upon these ridges long ago. No one knows for sure."

They were graceful, ethereal, yet more real than anything I had ever seen. Still, I could not believe they were truly there. I needed proof. I needed to feel the texture of their manes under my hands. I wondered, could I ride one if I wished? The wind hit me in gusts, and I knew that higher up, the same wind touched those magical stallions. It touched Zav and it touched Eytan. I felt I could fly if I wished. I felt—

"What was that?" I cried.

"What?"

"N-nothing." I turned a circle. "I thought I saw ..."

"Saw what?"

"A shadow. Some darkness." I scanned the sky and the snowy mountains. I shook my head. Whatever I had seen had disappeared without a trace. It had seemed so vivid moments ago, but now I could not even picture it, could not put it into words. I shivered again, and this time it was not from the cold. "It was nothing," I said firmly. "A trick of the light."

"If you're sure," Eytan said slowly, but he scanned our surroundings nonetheless, his demeanor shifting into something defensive.

We did not linger long in the mountains, mostly because I could not keep my teeth from chattering, or keep myself from complaining. In any case, we had seen the horses, and I was ready for our next adventure—hopefully somewhere with less snow.

Eytan proposed we travel next to Firth. I did not know if Firth was a city, a town, a castle, a river, or something else entirely, but I agreed without question, for fear of looking foolish, and we set off. I came to understand the extent of Eytan's wealth as we frequented inn after inn, stopping along the road only when the setting sun made it a necessity. He seemed unconcerned about the coin he was spending. In some places, the innkeepers and townsfolk already knew his name. When I voiced my observations, he would shrug and brush the question off. Perhaps it should have worried me, but I had my secrets as well, and he had treated me honorably thus far.

In any case, to part ways would leave me with only two options: make my way in this wide world alone, or return home and face what I had left behind. I knew that I was being selfish, but my fear of the witch remained, and in any case, I could not imagine facing my father now, not after what I had done. Besides, there was still more to see, and, if I were honest with myself, I wanted Eytan to be the one to show it to me.

* * * *

CHAPTER SEVEN

* * * *

We had just reached the base of the mountains, and I had just begun to regain feeling in my extremities, when we saw them. At first, I could not understand what I was seeing. It looked like a line of ants upon the horizon, but slower-moving, varying in shapes and sizes like great, hunched, charcoal smudges against the sky.

Eytan frowned. "I wonder what befell them."

I squinted against the sun. It was then that I realized I was looking at people: a long line of them, some carrying packs and bundles, others carrying children, some limping and staggering, others leading animals or pushing small carts.

"Where are they going?" I asked.

Eytan shrugged. "Hard to tell. They appear to be refugees. Perhaps their town was raided or destroyed, or perhaps their crops have failed. Or maybe they've just decided to resettle elsewhere."

"People do that?" I wondered aloud. "Simply pick up and move?"

"Of course. If something happens to their homes—a flood or a blight on their crops or tainted water or marauders or a thousand other things—they have no choice." He spoke gently, patiently, but without condescension. I was grateful for that. I knew I must seem terribly stupid to Eytan, to everyone.

"But where will they go?" I asked.

Eytan looked at me, and there was something very kind in his eyes. I would have called it admiration if there was anything in me to admire. "Would you like to find out?" he asked.

I nodded.

We made our way towards the line of people. As we approached them, I could see that some of them looked as if they would collapse at any moment. They swayed on their feet, their eyes listless. Some stared resolutely ahead, seemingly unwilling to admit exhaustion. Others moved throughout the line, encouraging others or helping them along.

It was one of these helpful travelers that Eytan approached. "Pardon," he said to a weary-looking woman who was, despite her exhaustion, loading other travelers' packs onto her cart. Her dark face was flushed with effort, her skin streaked with sweat and grime. "May I ask where you folk are journeying to?"

"You may ask," the woman said. She tossed thick black braids over her shoulder and hitched her cart up a bit, readjusting her grip.

"My lion could haul that for you a while," I offered. "If you'd like."

The woman shot me a look. "You think me weak?"

"No!" I could feel my cheeks growing hot. "No, I certainly didn't mean ... I just thought perhaps we could ..."

The woman managed a grim smile. "Sorry," she said. "Force of habit. I'd welcome a respite." She steered her cart toward me. Some others nearby seemed to drag themselves out of their stupors at the woman's movement, eyeing us with a mixture of wariness and curiosity. "All's well," the woman called to the travelers nearby. "Keep moving. It's all right." She turned back to us. "They have cause to be suspicious. Here, help me with this."

Together, we hitched the cart to Zav's shoulders, using a tack and harness that were already perched upon the cart's precarious pile. They had belonged to her mule, the woman told me, but the old beast had succumbed to exhaustion some days ago, and she had been forced to leave him on the path.

She held a rough, dirty hand out to me, and I shook it, irrationally ashamed of how clean and soft my own hands were.

"I'm Mandy. Our village elders ... couldn't make the journey, so I suppose I'm the leader of this little tribe." She was shaking Eytan's hand now.

"I am Eytan of Bahir," he told her, "and this is La—"

"Julia," I interjected. "And Zav." Zav shook his mane happily and continued to pull the cart, keeping pace with us easily. I tried to ignore Eytan's approving smile. He seemed impressed that I'd forced him to leave off the "Lady" in my name. I rolled my eyes at him.

"Well met," Mandy said.

"What is it that befell you?" I paused. "If you don't mind my asking."

Mandy shrugged. "What did *not* befall us? That would be a better question."

This piqued Eytan's interest. "How do you mean?"

Mandy swept her arm across the swath of ambling figures, trying to keep her expression hardened, but I could see the sadness in her eyes. Children had started to flit in and out of the line of the caravan, dancing close to Zav and then jumping back, shrieking in delight and fear. Mandy smiled at them.

"It was so sudden," she said, her face growing serious again. "It started with the first of our three elders. He disappeared in the night. We found his body four days later, at the entrance to the Eastern Wood, terribly mangled. I do not know what sort of creature could ..." She shook her head. "By the next week, our second elder was found dead in her bed. Her face was ... it was as if she had seen some great terror, and it had stopped her heart.

"Then, the crops began to fail, all of them at once. The potatoes, the wheat, the orchards, even down to the smallest vegetable garden. Everything was covered in blight or simply refused to grow. That's when the livestock started dying off."

"What could cause such a thing?" I asked, my voice hushed. I felt like I was listening to Annie's ghost stories again. I shuddered. I hoped that whatever had caused such misery in Mandy's village had not reached Annie's home.

Mandy shrugged. "Bad luck. Black magic. An angry god. Who can say?" She smiled again at the children, who had now gathered the courage to stroke Zav's mane and croon at him as he lumbered on. A little blond boy, a slip of a thing, so pale and thin he might have disappeared, was kissing Zav's nose repeatedly. Suddenly, there were tears in her eyes. "It was when the first child passed that we knew we could endure no longer. We packed everything we could carry and set off west. Our last elder was too frail to make the journey. She stayed behind to care for the village, in hopes that we might return one day." She wiped a tear from her cheek and grinned ruefully. "Mother always was stubborn."

A pang of guilt and grief struck me, making my stomach ache. I put a hand on Mandy's arm to stay her and, surprising her and myself, pulled her into an embrace. "I'm so sorry," I murmured into her thick braids.

That night, we helped Mandy's folk to make camp. Mandy introduced me to the village healer— a weathered old man with silver hair and milky eyes but a straight back, he seemed at once frail and powerful. He was also the tallest person I had ever seen. His height, his manner, the set of his jaw, all belied a wisdom I doubted I would ever obtain. Together, the healer, Mandy, and I visited the villagers who were ill or injured, giving them what care we could. I had no experience in the healing arts, but I had nursed my mother long enough at least to know how to soothe a person in distress.

In recent years especially, Mother had grown frail and listless; it seemed the sorrow that had long plagued her had finally worn so heavily upon her that she could see no other option than to succumb to it. Her sleep had always been troubled, but her nightmares had grown more and more frequent. Father would sometimes ask me to stay with her in the night, and when she awoke screaming, it was I who would comfort her, who would tell her all would be well, as her frenzied gaze searched the chambers for something that had long ago departed. So yes, I knew how to soothe.

I could feel tears pricking the backs of my eyes. I tried to put the thoughts of my mother from my head. Almost without my leave, my gaze sought Eytan. He was helping some of the other villagers prepare an evening meal, while simultaneously entertaining a large group of children. He stirred a large pot of stew over the fire with one hand, his free hand holding a skinny tree branch that he was using as a sword. He fenced with a little girl covered in freckles, who proudly wielded a much larger stick.

"Good!" he cried as she thrust and parried. "Make your opponent sweat! Never let up!"

"My arms are tired," the girl replied breathlessly.

Eytan's eyebrows shot up dramatically. "Then, by all means, let up! Anyway, supper is ready." He winked at the little girl. "I do believe you've earned the first helping."

I could not help smiling as I watched him spoon steaming ladles of soup into the children's bowls. We had been traveling together for two weeks now, but I felt as if I learned something new about him with each passing day.

The healer and I continued our work in comfortable silence, but after a few minutes, he nodded towards where Eytan now sat with a dozen children. They were huddled around a fire, sipping their soup, wide-eyed as Eytan told them stories, using his hands to make intricate shadow creatures dance along the side of a cart over his shoulder.

"He has a way with the children," the healer noted.

I smiled. "Yes, it would seem so."

"You are welcome to join them."

I hesitated. I had little experience with children. I had been just seven years old when my sister was born, and only ten when she died. Of course, I remembered how we used to play, the hours we spent racing through the halls of our manor, shrieking and giggling and gasping for breath as we played our games of pretend. Even as a toddler, she had been bolder than me, often proclaiming herself a pirate or a knight or a sorcerer. I was a princess, usually, or a mermaid, or a fairy whom little Julia was to save, or, occasionally, a dragon she had to battle.

We would dart into our mother's chambers and hassle her while she was at her needlepoint, or find her in the stables as she readied her horse for a canter around the grounds. She was always patient with us, always happy to be distracted. My mother taught me how to stitch tiny, delicate flowers. Meanwhile, my sister would roll an empty pin cushion across the floor, the way Zav would do years later, after my sister was gone but before Zav was fully grown. My mother—who, much to the servants' dismay, always insisted that if she were to ride a horse, she would also be the one to saddle him and care for him—taught us how to brush her dappled gray steed, lifting baby Julia up so she could reach.

On the rare occasions when my mother *did* need a respite from our antics, my father would take my sister and me into his study, rolling his eyes good-naturedly as we pulled books off of his shelves and examined the model ships he crafted within glass bottles.

I chuckled at the memory of a row Julia and I had had once in that study. She was just learning to speak in full sentences, and it had instilled a new agency in her that I found very frustrating. She had been brandishing one of my father's ships in a bottle, her chubby fingers wrapped around the bottle's neck.

"Daddy, I a pirate!" she had declared. "I've a sip"—she could not yet say "ship" properly—"I've a sip and I a pirate!" She had pointed a finger at me. "*You* a witch!"

"I'm not!" I had shouted. "I'm a beautiful mermaid. And you're ... well, you're just a fish!" I had struck the bottle from her hand, and it had rolled across the floor, knocking against the leg of my father's desk, where the glass cracked, the ship within shuddering in the tumult of my anger's storm.

Julia had wept inconsolably, convinced that I had killed her "sip." She had been comforted, I had been scolded, and I had been cold and resentful toward her for the next few days.

She had died less than a week later.

I bit the inside of my lip to keep from crying for the second time that day and told the healer, "I do not have a way with children."

* * * *

CHAPTER EIGHT

* * * *

Mandy's villagers did not have a destination in mind, so Eytan suggested that they journey west with us, towards Firth.

"There are folk there who will gladly aid you and your people," he assured her. "Perhaps you could found a new village there."

Mandy consulted with her people, and they agreed to travel with us a little farther. It seemed they were too weary to even consider any other options.

So we traveled west, and as we did, Eytan told the refugees stories of the rogues who inhabited the Firthen Forest. I was glad to learn what exactly we were headed towards, for I had remained too shy to ask. The outlaws of Firth, Eytan told us, robbed where they needed to and followed no law but their own. He promised us that they were harmless to folk like us, and he was certain they would be willing to help Mandy's people build a new village on the outskirts of their forest.

There were too many villagers in our caravan for all to enter the dense forest together, so Eytan and I helped them make camp in a clearing near its borders.

"The Firthen Forest is vast," Eytan told Mandy before we bid her farewell. "It may be several days before we make our way back to you with word. But your people will be safe here. Rest, recover. We will send provisions as soon as we can."

Mandy grasped his arm in thanks and then embraced me. I hugged her back. It felt natural now to show affection in this way. Then, she ruffled Zav's mane and waved us off. Eytan, Zav, and I continued into the Firthen Forest alone.

But once we were within the forest, surrounded by the stillness of the old trees and the sweet, rich smell of moss and undergrowth, I began to doubt whether the outlaws existed at all. We wandered through dense trees for three days, but the woods seemed empty, save a few small animals and birds.

Each time we stopped for sleep I had strange dreams: of the Wall, of the raven who had followed me through the woods Outside, of the shadow in the mountains. I dreamed that the raven and the shadow were one and the same. In my dreams, the creature grew vast, its wings stretching leagues and blotting out the sun. The shadows it cast over the land reached their tendrils outward from the forest that bordered my home. I could see those tendrils, dark and menacing and barbed with poisonous thorns, snaking their way into the villages surrounding the forest. They choked plants and livestock, shattered windows, and snuffed out hearth fires. I saw the shadows enter Annie's home, coiling around her family and squeezing the life out of them. I saw the shadows infiltrate an unfamiliar dwelling and wrap themselves around an old woman with dark skin and eyes just like Mandy's. I could hear their strangled screams. I awoke screaming too.

Eytan thought I was ill, and perhaps I was, but I knew there was no cure for my nightmares. Something was haunting me each time I closed my eyes.

On our fourth day in the forest, we stumbled across a hare caught in a trap. Zav looked at the creature hungrily, his tongue lolling out the side of his mouth, but I stayed him with a hand to his velvety nose. Eytan knelt beside the trap. The rabbit's frenzied eyes grew wider as Eytan drew near.

"Shh, little one. I won't hurt you," he said softly. He drew the blade from the sheath hidden within his boot and cut at the wooden trapping until it sprung apart. The hare darted away into the undergrowth. Eytan straightened. "There now," he said.

"That might have been someone's dinner," I told him.

"Indeed it was."

Eytan and I turned to face the man who had spoken. He was shockingly handsome, with tan skin, dark brown hair, and an angular face. Eytan was staring at the man as intently as I was, but he seemed far more concerned with the stranger's taut bow and sharpened arrow than with his strong jaw and perfect features.

"We meant no harm," Eytan said in the same tone he had used to calm the rabbit.

"Oh? As the lass said, that was dinner you just set loose, and the trap you ruined took me a good while to build. But since you meant no harm ..." The man pulled his elbow to his ear and squared his shoulders, and I watched in terror as he loosed his arrow.

My scream did not sound until the arrow had flown. Zav roared, Eytan darted aside, and a glint of sunlight through the trees reflected off of something in the air, blinding me for a moment. I recovered, grabbed Eytan by the shoulder, and ran my hands along his chest, searching for where the arrow had pierced him, but he was unharmed. He took my hands and lowered them, regarding the stranger calmly.

"How—" the man began, but the cry of a bird interrupted him. I looked up to see a silver falcon swooping through the sky, the stranger's arrow in its talons. Eytan extended his arm, and the falcon perched on his leather sleeve.

"Where have you been?" Eytan asked the bird sternly. He took the arrow from its beak and tossed the splintered wood over his shoulder. Stroking the falcon's shining feathers, Eytan continued, "I have been worried about you, you know. Little scoundrel. How many times have I told you? Vanishing for weeks at a time, it's no way to behave."

The falcon cooed happily.

"Eytan?" I prompted, for our would-be attacker still had a good many arrows left in his quiver, and I did not doubt he would use them.

Eytan looked up. "Oh, yes. You are an outlaw of Firth, are you not?"

"I am," the man replied proudly.

"You must be a fresh recruit. I am well respected by the outlaws. My name is Eytan of Bahir."

Recognition flashed across the man's face, followed by a flush of color and a look of absolute chagrin. "Of course! Sir, I am sorry. Please, you are welcome here."

Eytan inclined his head. "Thank you. Now, I do hope rabbit is not the only food to be had around here. My companions and I are very hungry, but you may have heard that the Midbari do not eat the flesh of animals."

The man nodded profusely and led us toward his camp.

As we walked, I muttered, "I thought you told me they were harmless."

Eytan simply shrugged as I scowled.

The camp was a cluster of flimsy wooden structures built around the trees, flanked by a slope of land on one side and a river on the other, with a fire pit in the center. Our stranger, who introduced himself as Sladan, led us through a maze of workbenches and barrels of food and drink to a large central tent filled with men setting down plates of food.

At the entrance to the tent, Sladan shouted, "My kin!"

Dozens of heads shot up, and a roar went through the mass. "Eytan!" some yelled as others cheered.

"Our friends are hungry!" Sladan proclaimed, and before I could blink, I was swept into the tent and placed at a head table beside Eytan. Outlaws swarmed around us, serving wine and offering up meats (which Eytan refused), thick bread, and vegetables still steaming from their fires. Soon, the clamor died down, and Eytan and I were left to eat in relative peace.

It was as if a sudden rainstorm had come and gone, leaving me drenched and shivering even as the sun returned to the sky. But Eytan made no explanations and no introductions, so I simply resigned myself to my confusion and ate.

"Why is it that you do not eat meat?" I asked finally, unsure why this was the detail I had seized upon.

"My religion considers it a sin to eat that which was once alive. Instead, it asks us to treat our fellow beings as equals, which is why I've made certain Zav and Falcon will be fed well."

I laughed.

"What?" Eytan asked.

"You've named your falcon 'Falcon'?"

"I lack the creative energies you seem to have in such abundance."

"May I ask you something?" I said.

"You mean something *else*?"

I sighed. It seemed Eytan became more sardonic the more familiar we became. "Why did you want me to meet the outlaws?"

"They are good people who have been given a bad reputation. I thought you might want to meet such individuals. It could help you see the world for what it is."

"That is a very philosophical answer," I said, "but a lie, I think."

Eytan seemed impressed. "You know, for someone who has not known the world very long, you are very perceptive."

I blushed, though I was not sure why.

"The leader of these people has been a good friend to me, and I am in need of counsel. That is why we have come."

I wondered what counsel Eytan could need. He seemed so self-assured. But I did not press. Instead, I said, "And you thought I would like them."

"You will." Eytan smiled mischievously. "Just wait until you hear them sing!"

The outlaws of Firth were young and old, men and women, of every race, color, background, and creed, but they all held one common quality: they could not sing. As we sat around the common fire that night, drink, fruits, and sweetmeats were served as rowdy, wine-warmed outlaws began to sing a ballad about a sailor and his best fish:

The sailor he had a wish, a wish
(a wish, a wish, a wish he had)

For the best of all the fish, the fish
(the fish, the fish, the fish he had)
So he took with him a fine young lad
(a lad, a lad, a lad he took)
And he searched and he scoured and he told the lad
(the lad, the lad, the lad he told)
That it would make the most succulent dish, dish, dish!

Despite their caterwauling and drunken revelry, I found that Eytan was right—I did like them. I could not say I approved of their ways, but they stole only from the wealthy and harmed none. And they were cheerful and confident, singing off-key with abandon and laughing as if they hadn't a care in the world. These people lived a life of constant danger, and yet, they showed no worry, no fear. Just camaraderie and dedication. As the evening wore on and raucous singing turned to soft conversation, I leaned against Eytan's shoulder, drowsy from drink and travel, and I began to feel a strange, comfortable sensation come over me. I thought that, perhaps, it was the feeling of home.

I slept with Zav in a private tent the outlaws had set up for me. Within the tent was a sleeping mat piled high with furs and cushions. It was the most comfortable sleeping arrangement I had had since we'd encountered Mandy and her refugees many days before, and I felt guilty for feeling so relieved by it. Still, I settled in to sleep, curled against Zav's warm flank. I dreamed again of the Wall, but this time, my dreams were calmer, and when I awoke to the sounds of outlaws performing their morning chores, I felt well-rested for the first time in weeks.

I emerged from my tent wondering if there was breakfast to be had, and found Eytan reclining against a tree trunk just outside, whittling away at a piece of wood.

"Good morning, m'lady," he said smoothly, without looking up at me.

"Good morning," I replied.

"The outlaws have asked me to fetch some eggs for them. Would you care to join me?"

"I suppose, but—"

"Come on then!" Eytan had already risen and was striding away, still whittling as he walked. I rolled my eyes, collected my skirts, and followed, wishing he was not quite so abrupt.

As we walked, I savored the beauty of the forest. The morning sun was barely high enough to reach the trees, but shafts of low light made the underbrush come alive. Sunlight dappled my feet with green and gold and illuminated tiny flowers. Purple, blue, white, and yellow petals swayed in the breeze, and the entire forest smelled of their sweet breath. Birds, just awakening from their slumbers, fluttered overhead, chirping giddily as they searched for insects or seeds. I became so enthralled that I did not notice Eytan had stopped walking until I ran into him.

"Why have we stopped?" I asked, collecting myself and blushing yet again. Had I been prone to this inside the Wall? I could not quite remember. It had only been a matter of weeks since I had left, but it seemed a lifetime ago.

Eytan pointed. "There."

I looked up to see a large nest laden with half a dozen eggs.

Eytan began to climb the tree, and I had the distinct impression he was showing off for me. But climbing proved a difficult feat, as the tree was straight and tall, with no branches to use as hand- or footholds.

"Well," I said, "you'll have to pick a better tree than that." I scanned the area. Nearby, I spied another nest-adorned tree. This one was shorter and a bit crooked. I made my way up the mountainous roots and used a low-hanging branch to haul myself up. I hoisted myself up to the next branch, tested its weight, and crawled out onto it. I tucked my dress underneath me and waved down to Eytan.

"When did a lady learn to climb trees?"

"When did a desert dweller?"

"Fair point." He hopped down from his tree and began to climb mine.

"We had a few fair climbing trees within the Wall. It was the best way to get a view beyond it." I flashed him a smile. "I am an excellent climber." Inching out along my branch, I finally reached the nest I had spotted from the ground. "How do we get the eggs down without breaking them?" I asked.

"Hand me one."

I squeaked in surprise at Eytan's voice so close to my ear. He had crept up right behind me. Startled, I began to fall sideways and my heart seemed to skip a beat until Eytan pulled me back and held me securely on the branch.

I put a hand to my chest and took a few deep breaths to slow my racing heart.

"Do *not*," I panted, "sneak up on me so!"

Eytan chuckled, but he kept his arm around my waist to hold me steady. I felt my cheeks grow hot and fought to ignore the strange fluttering in my stomach.

"Are you all right?" he asked.

I sighed irritably. "Yes," I replied. "Now, let go. I am going to get that egg." I stretched my arm as far as I could, picked up a delicate blue egg, and passed it to Eytan.

"Perfect," he said. "Would you like to see something beautiful?" He held the egg above his head. The sun was rising higher, and as Eytan found a patch of light, the egg became translucent.

"Oh," I whispered. The sun beat through the egg, and I could see a shadow of liquid that swirled vaguely when Eytan's hand moved.

"You see?" Eytan asked. "The shell is so thin that when the light comes through it, you can see an outline of what's inside. My father taught me that trick a long time ago."

I searched his face. That was the first personal detail he had told me. I wondered if he was beginning to open up to me, or if he had just forgotten himself in the moment. He did not notice me looking, though—or if he did, he gave no indication. Instead, he slipped the egg into a pouch at his waist, his gaze focused on the branch he was straddling.

He almost looked nervous. I wondered if he actually had much experience in climbing trees. Perhaps he'd only done it to impress me. The thought made me blush, and I quickly turned back to the nest and picked up another egg, hoping Eytan had not seen my cheeks redden.

I passed Eytan egg after egg, and he secured them in his pouch. When we had emptied the nest, we descended, careful not to break our treasures, and headed back to the camp.

"When will we ask the outlaws for aid?" I asked. "For Mandy and her people?"

"I'll discuss it when the outlaws' leader returns." He gave me that same look that he had worn when I'd stopped him from revealing to Mandy that I was a lady, the look that was almost admiration. "You needn't worry. We should be able to settle all of that soon."

We took the eggs back to the outlaws, and one of the men who had served us the night before taught me how to cook them in a pan over an open flame. He even showed me the best herbs to add to the mixture. I took my first bite and tasted heaven, and my heart swelled with pride. Somehow, the food tasted better because I had had a hand in making it.

Still, I felt melancholy. I had met so many new people, but I was no closer to finding the Lion Boy. Perhaps I should have let Eytan take me directly to Midbar in the first place. Perhaps it would not have made a difference. I wondered if it was time I stopped fixating on a boy I would likely never find. The world was vaster than I had ever imagined. Maybe it was enough that I was here in it.

* * * * *

CHAPTER NINE

* * * *

We stayed with the outlaws for two more nights and were treated unrelentingly as royalty. On our third morning in the Firthen Forest, I watched a tall young woman I did not recognize stride into the village. She shook off her hood as if shaking off water after a long rain, and her mane of orange hair shone like a beacon beneath the strong sun. She smiled casually at the forest at large, and the smile lit up her entire face. She was dressed all in greens, even down to her boots, her quiver, her bow, and her arrows. I watched her saunter confidently through the mess of tools that littered the campsite but said nothing, trying to be invisible.

Unfortunately, I was the only person in the camp, a point on which I was still sore. Eytan had left me behind while he prowled the roads with the outlaws, and thus, I had determined never to speak to him again. This left me easy to spot in the empty camp, especially since Zav lay beside me, snoring unabashedly. And spot me the stranger did. Her eyes fell upon me, and a quizzical expression passed over her face.

"Hullo," she said.

For a moment, I considered fleeing to my tent, but instead, I murmured, "Hello."

"Well, now. I haven't had a lady in my camp for some time now. Who brought you here?"

"Eytan," I replied, my cheeks burning at the woman's use of the word "lady." I was beginning to despise how obvious that seemed to people. "Of Bahir."

The woman raised an eyebrow and chuckled. "The rascal."

"*Your* camp?" I asked.

"Indeed. I'm called Wren Farley, and I founded this camp. And what is your name?"

"Lady Julia." I had told the lie so many times it had begun to feel like the truth.

"Lady Julia." Wren Farley swept into a low bow, then she walked to me and kissed my hand. "It is a pleasure."

I had never been kissed by a woman before, aside from the wet, happy kisses my mother had planted on my cheeks when I was young. "Likewise," I murmured.

"And what brings you to the Firthen Forest?"

I was speechless for a moment, for I realized I did not know what I was doing there. Although I tried not to dwell on it too often, the truth was I had no idea why I was wandering around with a man I hardly knew. I had no idea why I had even left the Wall.

Farley chuckled, folding her arms across her chest and leaning against a tree. "Don't fret. It wasn't a trick question."

"I ... I'm just not certain."

Farley shrugged and linked arms with me, causing my stomach to drop a bit with a nervousness I did not understand. Her face was very close to mine now, and I blushed again. She was not beautiful, exactly, but she was striking.

"Come," she said, leading me into the forest, "let's take a walk." I looked back at Zav. "He'll be fine. Let sleeping lions lie, eh?" She paused for a moment and then said, more softly, "You know, it's all right not to know."

I did not know what to say to that, so I simply nodded, feeling foolish. We walked a while longer until the trees grew dense around us.

"Where are we going?" I asked.

"I don't know! See how easy that was?"

I laughed in spite of myself.

"You know the brilliant thing about this forest? She never lets you lose your way." Farley paused and looked at me. "It seems to me you've lost your way. Maybe Firth can help you find it."

"Can it do that?"

"Of course she can. But you've got to find yourself first."

I hung my head. "I don't know if I can."

"You can," Farley told me. "You just don't know it yet."

"Lady Farley?"

"I'm no Lady. Call me Wren."

"Wren. How ... how did *you* find yourself?"

Wren looked up and smiled. I followed her gaze and found that we were somehow back at the camp. The outlaws were returning from their plundering and the camp was abuzz with activity. Wren's features had taken on a look of pure contentment, and when she said, "I had help," I knew exactly what she meant.

"So," Eytan said.

"So," I replied. It was midday, and we were waiting for Wren to come back from an errand so we could ask her about Mandy and the villagers.

"I see you've met Wren."

"Yes." I thought for a moment. "I like her."

Eytan laughed. "What human with eyes in their skull doesn't?"

I shook my head. "That's not—oh. You were joking."

"I was. Wren is a dear friend of mine. She taught me my skill at the bow, you know. I have known her for a long time. Long enough to know that there is more to her than her good looks and her roguish ways. They shall write songs about her deeds someday."

"You admire her very much."

"She's done much for me." Eytan stretched, keenly reminding me of a cat, and rested his head on a tree trunk. He absently stroked Falcon, who was perched on his knee.

"I love this forest," Eytan said, more to himself than to me. "I think I could stay here for my whole life." He chuckled. "If only." He was smiling, but there was a note of bitterness in his voice.

"Then why don't you?"

"I have responsibilities. Soon I shall have to return to Bahir and take my place."

I leaned forward, sensing an opportunity to learn more about the parts of himself Eytan kept hidden. "Your place?"

"In the family. Oh, there's Wren!" Eytan sprung up, and I was sure he was avoiding my question. I narrowed my eyes but followed him to speak with her.

"Eytan," she said as we approached. "I am enjoying getting to know your friend." She winked then, though I was not sure why.

"Now, Wren," Eytan said, a note of playful warning in his voice.

"What? I'm only being friendly!"

Eytan rolled his eyes. "That's what you always say."

I was utterly perplexed, but I supposed that a friendship as old as Eytan and Wren's was bound to have some private jests. They were strolling together now, and I followed them into Wren's large tent, where she welcomed us to sit around a rough-hewn wooden table and poured us sweet wine.

We sat with the leader of the outlaws and discussed Mandy and her people for some time. Wren shook her head sadly as we finished explaining all the misfortunes that had befallen the villagers.

"I've heard talk from the east," she said, her voice low.

Once more, the feeling of telling ghost stories overtook me. I rubbed my arms to rid myself of the gooseflesh that had risen on my skin despite the warm air.

"What sort of talk?" Eytan asked.

"Nothing quite so terrible as what your friends have experienced. But there have been ... queer happenings. Disappearances. Animals behaving oddly. Vines and brambles suddenly overgrown on otherwise clear roads." She shrugged.

"Probably just stories."

Still, I could tell she was perturbed. "What about here in Firth?" I asked. "Have there been any happenings here?"

Wren grinned. "Oh no, we're terribly boring here. Your Mandy and her people will be quite safe." She stood. "I'll send Sladan and some of the others to bring your friends some supplies. We'll organize work parties to help them build shelters and such over the next few weeks as well. There's plenty of time before winter." Wren met my gaze. "We'll get them settled. Don't worry."

"Thank you."

She held out a hand to me then, and I took it without hesitating.

Smiling, she said, "Now then, Eytan. I'm going to steal Julia away for a while. You went off plundering without her, I hear. So now we shall have our own fun without you."

I had never seen such a look of bewilderment on Eytan's face.

Wren led me to a clearing in the forest, where several bales of hay had been painted with targets. On a tree nearby leaned several bows and quivers full of arrows.

"Now then, Julia, would you like to try your hand at a bow and arrow?"

I beamed. "I very much would!"

She handed me a bow and situated herself behind me, pressing her body against my back as she positioned my arms properly. Again, my cheeks grew hot. I let my hair fall into my face, grateful that my russet waves could hide my blush. I could not understand why everything she did flustered me so.

Wren did not seem to notice. She wrapped her fingers around my left hand, positioning my fingers properly and then tightening my grip on the bow. Her hands were calloused but warm. I wondered what it would feel like to hold her hand, not for a purpose, but simply to hold and be held.

"Hold fast," she said in my ear as if she had heard my thoughts, "and knock your arrow."

Her right arm reached around my other side, settling the arrow into place. The wood was smooth against my fingers, and I felt suddenly powerful, more confident than I had just a moment before. She took my right hand in hers and brought it to the bowstring, then guided my arm backward until my elbow was at my ear.

"I'm going to let go of the string now," she said. "You'll have to hold on very tight. It's more difficult than it seems."

I nodded and said nothing, concentrating on keeping my body positioned as Wren had instructed, but also noticing how pleasant her soft breath felt against my cheek. But as she removed her hands from mine, all thoughts of Wren left my mind and were replaced by a sudden, desperate cry from my muscles as I struggled to keep the bowstring taut. She had warned me, but the amount of strength it took was still far more than I had expected. My arms were already trembling.

"You were not joking," I said through gritted teeth.

She laughed a laugh that sounded like birdsong, but also somehow like the singing of an arrow being loosed. Perhaps that was just my imagination, desperate for me to loose the arrow I now held.

"Go on, then," she said. "Let go."

And I did.

It was an incredible feeling. The relief in my muscles as I let the arrow fly, the snap of the bowstring, the whistle of the arrow, and then the *twang* as it drove itself into the trunk of a tree, even the sweat on my brow, they were all intoxicating. I did not even care that I had missed my mark; the hay bale was far to the right of the tree from which my arrow now protruded, but it did not matter. I had loosed an arrow. My fingers, my arms, my muscles had caused it to fly.

I whirled towards Wren, dropping the bow in my excitement and launching myself onto the tips of my toes to fling my arms around her neck. "I did it!" I cried.

Laughing, she wrapped her arms around my waist. "You did at that." Keeping one hand at the small of my back, she stopped to grab my bow. "Let's see if we can't hit the target this time," she added, but there was no judgment in her tone, and her encouraging smile sent warmth spreading across my chest.

We practiced all afternoon, and by the time the sun was setting, I was drenched in sweat, with my hair plastered to my forehead, my fingertips stinging, and my arms aching. But I had hit the target enough times that Wren seemed genuinely impressed.

"Not bad for your first day of practice," she said. "Not bad at all. Now, come on. There is a hot spring nearby. We can clean ourselves up before supper."

We peeled off our sweat-stained clothes and draped them over tree branches to air them out, then climbed into the scalding water of the spring, our skin turning pink from the heat. I didn't mind it, though. It felt soothing on my sore muscles, and the fact that Wren had brought me to this place made me feel special somehow, chosen.

She leaned her head back and dipped her long hair into the water, running her fingers through it to cleanse it of grime, so I did the same. It was not quite a real bath, but it was the cleanest I had felt in some time. Since before we had visited the Northern Mountains, Eytan and I had been bathing in streams, taking turns splashing icy water on ourselves while the other kept a polite distance.

This was certainly preferable.

"I suppose you and Eytan will be moving on soon," Wren said. Her eyes were closed, but I had a feeling she was only feigning nonchalance.

"I suppose so," I said. "We are looking for someone, you see. Well, looking and exploring."

"The Lion Boy." Wren smiled. "Eytan told me. He must be very special for you to travel so far and wide in search of him."

I hesitated. "Honestly, I'm not so sure." I trailed my finger over the surface of the water, watching the steam dance around my skin. "I started this journey in search of him, but I know how unlikely it is I'll succeed in finding him. And now that I am out here—in the world, I mean—I am not sure failing would be such a bad thing."

"Why is that?"

"I have learned and seen so much, and ..." I chanced a glance at her face, but that only made the blush return to my cheeks. I hoped the heat of the spring would mask it. I continued, "I have met so many wonderful people. Even if I never find the Lion Boy, I've already gained so much."

Wren smiled again, and I decided she was beautiful after all, especially when she smiled. "Well," she said, standing. She offered me her hand. "It seems to me you are well on your way to finding yourself."

We dressed and began to stroll back to the camp together. The sun had set, but the moon was almost full, and it shone so brightly through the trees that I could see the path laid out before me clearly. Besides, Wren knew these woods. I felt safe by her side.

Something nagged at me as we walked, like I had forgotten something, but there was nothing to forget. It felt almost as if there was something I was meant to do, something that I needed to do before it was too late. I was puzzling over this when Wren's fingers brushed my own. At first, I thought it was a mistake, but then she edged closer, and her fingers lingered against mine.

We walked hand in hand towards the camp, our steps slowing until Wren paused behind a great, wide tree, her eyes very bright in the moonlight as she looked closely at my face. I could neither have predicted nor explained what happened next, but before I could stop myself, before I could overthink or worry about decorum or manners, I turned towards Wren and raised myself up once more onto the tips of my toes to reach her height. But this time, I did not wrap my arms around her. This time, I did something I had never done before. There in the night, awash in moonlight, amidst the trees of her forest, I kissed Wren Farley, and she returned the kiss.

Her soft lips tasted mildly of salt, but there was a sweetness beneath that, and I was certain it was the best thing I had ever tasted. We stayed like that for several minutes, I on the tips of my toes, she with her chin ducked to meet my lips, our fingers intertwined. I was blushing again, but this time I did not care.

The next day dawned clear and crisp, with more of a chill than there had been in the days preceding it. It was as if the world knew that it was time to say goodbye. It was time for us to move on.

Wren and her outlaws gathered to bid us farewell.

Sladan was beside her. "Mandy and her people are well," he told me. "She told me to tell you 'thank you.'"

"Thank *you*," I replied. I turned my gaze to Wren, who was grinning at me, a bit mischievously, I thought. "And thank you as well," I told her.

"Of course," she said softly. Then, to Eytan, "Your visits are consistently too short." She shook his hand, and then she pulled Eytan into an embrace. "You will always be welcome here, brother."

Eytan clapped Wren on the back. "And believe me, I shall take advantage of the invitation as often as possible. You know I can't resist a free meal."

Wren chuckled and mussed up Eytan's dark hair. "If you ever need anything—"

"I won't hesitate to find you," Eytan assured her. "And likewise. Should there ever be the need—"

"I know how to reach you."

I tried to leave the two to their farewells, but Wren would have none of that. After giving Eytan's shoulder a final squeeze, she swept into one of her graceful, outlandish bows, letting her fiery hair fall into her face.

"My lady," she said, "you are welcome in Firth whenever your heart may desire its company, or ours. I hope you might find your way back here, after you've found yourself."

I nodded. "I am sure I shall," I told her, and I meant it with all my heart.

CHAPTER TEN

✳ ✳ ✳ ✳ ✳

✳ ✳ ✳ ✳ ✳

Sladan escorted Zav, Eytan, Falcon, and me from the forest, and once we were back on a road and my spirits were high from a goodbye full of promise and visits to come, I asked, "So, where to now?"

"The Singing Mountains," Eytan replied, but something in his voice told me that was the last place he wished to go. He forced a cheerful note into his voice. "There is a temple there where we will be welcome. I believe you will like it."

I raised an eyebrow. "Is that the only reason?"

He managed a smile, but I could see that it was false. "I've had a message. An emissary is waiting for me there. Sent by my father."

"Do you need to return to Bahir?"

"No, nothing like that. If I make an appearance, my father should be satisfied. Then, we can continue on our way. Besides, you truly will like the temple."

I nodded, knowing that there was something weighing on Eytan's heart, and struggling not to let him see what was weighing on mine.

Our journey took us through towns and villages full of interesting people and exciting trades. I watched in awe as a Midbari man juggled fire in one village, and I wondered at the exotic jewels a dark-skinned trader with an infectious smile sold in the next town. Eytan bought me a flower like none I had ever seen at a market along the way. He called it a lotus and laughed when I nestled it in Zav's mane.

I heard snatches of speech in strange tongues and saw people and clothing both beautiful and foreign. I listened intently to every language I heard, trying to pick up words and phrases. I wondered at the exquisiteness of things that did not seem to impress Eytan at all. As we reached the base of the Singing Mountains, flurries of snow drifting around us and settling in Eytan's dark hair, I knew I never wanted to return to the Wall.

I was nearly asleep when we reached the temple. Four days of traveling in the mountains had made me weary. It was more than that, though. I had grown more and more tired of late, the currents of sleep constantly trying to pull me under. I snuggled my face into Zav's mane to keep warm as he carried me up the winding mountain trail, Eytan moving steadily before us. My eyelids drooped further and further closed as Eytan pounded on the giant wooden front gate of the Temple of Song.

I watched blearily as a man in a robe opened the gates, bowed to Eytan, and led us in. I absentmindedly admired the patterns of the stones in the courtyard beyond, trying in vain to trace the winding designs. I paid no mind as Zav loped up the steps to the main doors of the temple, where we waited for the man who had closed the gate behind us to make his way up to the doors. Finally, he pulled them open for us, and as the heavy wooden doors swung inward, the most wonderful smell I had ever smelled wafted into my nostrils, and the most glorious music I had ever heard greeted my ears. We had come to the Temple of Song.

I wanted to keep my eyes open then. I wanted to see the rich colors and textures of the temple; the mahogany and crimson and gold. I wanted to find the source of the heady scents that surrounded me and the sweet sounds that caressed my ears. But I was too close to sleep to fight very hard, and soon I was overcome by a strange tilting sensation. A moment too late, I realized I was slipping from Zav's back, but before I could be bothered to open my eyes, I felt myself being cradled against something warm. I laid my head against it and drifted to sleep.

I was kneeling at the bank of a stream, setting wildflowers afloat in little rafts made of leaves. My father was calling for me.

"Julia! Julia, come inside."

I ignored him, too involved with my seafaring flowers. They were going to journey far and wide, like in the stories Father always told us.

I saw her reflection in the clear water before I saw her. Whirling around, I stared into her eyes.

"I am looking for something," she told me, her expression remote. She seemed strange, but familiar. As if, with a twist of her features, she could be someone I knew. "Won't you help me find it?"

"Julia!" my father called.

I wanted to glance toward the manor, to see if he was coming, but I could not tear my gaze away from her.

Her mouth twitched. "That is a lie."

"What?" I heard my faint voice ask.

"You are not her," the woman said, her voice harsh. And only then did I know her. My mother's face hardened. "You are not my Julia."

I blinked against the white light of a snowy dawn, disoriented. Had I been dreaming? I vaguely remembered the sensation of falling ... I sat up quickly. I was in the Temple of Song! The thrill of adventure chased away the remaining wisps of the dream, and I sprung from my bed. I looked down at myself. Someone—Eytan, I presumed—had removed my cloak and boots, hanging the former over a chair and placing the latter by the side of the bed. My dress was wrinkled and dirty from traveling. I sighed. Washing it in streams and rivers was less than satisfactory for my taste. Before I'd left the Wall, I had never done my own washing.

There was a wardrobe at the far end of the room. Worrying I wasn't meant to look inside, but hoping there was something I could wear within, I opened the door, and gasped. It seemed there were hundreds of dresses; velvet and satin and beads and lace flowed out towards me in rich, royal shades and in soft spring hues. I bit my lip. Were these for me?

I could not be sure, so I dug into the back of the wardrobe and found a simple, roughspun brown dress. I shrugged out of the fine wool dress I had worn for weeks and into the shift that might not have been meant for me, struggling to lace it without the help of servants. We had been traveling for so long now, but every time I dressed myself, my hands felt clumsy, and I felt ashamed. I should have been able to do such things without help long ago. How sheltered I had been, and in so many ways. I donned my cape, tugged my boots on, and stepped out of my room into a long hall awash in sunlight. My brow furrowed. The light streamed in from windows set into the hallway's ceiling, and the walls were paneled in layered wood that could be doors or decorations. I could see no end to the hall in either direction.

"Hello?" I called. "Hello? Anyone? Hel—" I fell silent at the sight of a monk standing a ways down the hall.

The monk flashed me a slight smile and turned away, shuffling down the hall. I supposed he meant for me to follow, so I did. As we walked, I could hear faint music from behind the walls of the hallway. Suddenly, I realized why it seemed that the hallway had no end. It was curving. We walked for so long I thought we must have made a full circuit, but then we arrived at a golden archway I had not seen before, set into the outward curve of the hall. The monk led me through it, out onto a platform dappled in sunlight that streamed through a woven awning. There, Eytan was leaning over the balcony's railing, his hair blowing in the wintry wind. Falcon circled in the air beyond.

"Good morning," I said.

Eytan turned to me, his smile mirroring mine.

"How did you sleep?" he asked, his arms clasped behind his back.

"Fine," I replied, breathless because it was cold, and because he was standing so close, and because I was lying.

His eyes searched mine, and I could tell he had heard the falsehood in my single word.

"The nightmares?"

I nodded.

Eytan looked up and nodded, acknowledging the monk who had brought me. The monk was setting a tray of food upon a rug scattered with pillows. I had not even noticed his departure or return.

"Sit," Eytan offered. "Eat. You'll feel better."

I complied and picked at a slice of sweet bread. Eytan poured me tea, which I drank. It warmed my chest. Eytan watched me intently, and for a long time, neither of us spoke.

Finally, Eytan murmured, "I had nightmares when I was small."

I looked up at him and waited for him to continue.

"You see, my father is a powerful man. And powerful men are always in danger. From envious men, from greedy men, from men who would take power not theirs to take. And as the son of a powerful man, I was also in danger. When I was seven, a man stole into our home and tried to kill me. It was the ultimate way to hurt my father since I am his only son. I stand to inherit his power, and I have all his love." Eytan spread his arms. "Obviously, the assassin failed. But, he came close. Far too close. And for a long time, I was terrified to close my eyes at night. That's why I learned to defend myself. So I understand. I know what it's like to be afraid of your own mind."

"I'm so sorry that happened to you," I said. I smiled weakly. "And thank you," I added.

We sat in silence for a while longer, until I broke it with a laugh as Falcon landed on my shoulder. I fed him some of my sweet bread.

Eytan pulled one knee up to his chest and slung his arm over his leg. "Maybe you should give him a name," he suggested. "A proper name, I mean."

I glanced up, surprised. "Really? You wouldn't mind?"

Eytan shrugged. "It's not up to me. But, he wouldn't mind, I don't think."

I held out my arm and let Falcon inch down it until he grasped my wrist.

"Well?" I asked the bird. "What do you say? Do you fancy a proper name?"

Falcon crooned at me.

Laughing, I stroked his beak thoughtfully. "Kes," I decided. "His name is Kes."

"Moonbeam," Eytan murmured.

I nodded.

"Kes and Zav. Moon and sun. Silver and gold." Eytan smiled. "I like it. It has symmetry." He took a sip of his tea, eyeing me playfully.

"What?" I asked when I could hold out under his gaze no longer.

He broke into an impish grin. "Want to learn to sing?"

I followed Eytan down a stairway I had not noticed before and out into the rock gardens below. There, dozens of monks sat cross-legged upon the smooth, cold stones, their gold and crimson robes billowing in the wind. I could not explain it, but I felt this was the most beautiful thing I had seen in my travels yet. As I stared, Eytan took a seat, folding his legs beneath him. He beckoned for me to sit beside him.

"I don't hear any singing," I hissed in his ear.

He laughed softly. "Close your eyes. Wait. Listen."

I sighed. "Very well." I closed my eyes and strained my ears to hear something besides the wind. I waited until the stone made my backside sore and cold, and then I waited longer.

Soon, thoughts of my mother crept into my head. I fought to keep them out, but they were persistent. Some were happy—memories of my mother laughing or singing, or carrying my sister in her arms, with me leading them through the hedge maze on the grounds within the Wall. But others were dark and murky and made me feel as if I were drowning. I shivered. I felt a large hand slip into mine, and I opened one eye. Eytan's eyes were still closed, but his face seemed determined, as if he were deeply concentrated on my hand. I squeezed his and closed my eyes once more.

With my hand warm and safe in Eytan's, my thoughts were peaceful, and not even the biting winter wind bothered me. I waited patiently now, concentrating on my breathing and the feel of Eytan's calloused skin. After a while, I felt myself blushing, but even that did not perturb me. And then I heard it. First, it was so soft and low I thought perhaps it was the wind, but then it grew louder and richer. Soon, another sound joined the first one, then another, then another, and finally, there seemed to be a hundred different notes. They wove in and out of a melody so complex I could barely follow it, and I realized that I was humming along with the monks.

To my surprise, my tune mixed flawlessly with the others drifting around me. After a time, I could not tell which tune was mine, and which belonged to Eytan and to the monks. I opened my eyes to find Eytan staving off a grin as he hummed, his eyes still closed. I flicked his forehead with the hand that was not nestled in his, and his humming faltered. I stuck my tongue out, although he could not see me, and then continued humming until Eytan nudged me. I nudged him back, and the two of us struggled to stifle our laughter as the monks continued to sing.

The nightmares were worse than ever that night. I awoke more than once, wishing Zav was with me, but the monks had given him a stall in the stables. I dreamed that I was walking in a field of wildflowers, but as I pressed on, the flowers began to die. I knelt down to brush one with my fingers, and it turned to dust. I spun in a circle, horrified, as I watched the flowers wilt around me until the field was black with rot. I bolted awake from the dream, my heart racing. It was pitch black in my room, and I knew I could not have been asleep for long. I took a deep, ragged breath, and settled back to try to sleep again.

The next dream had me tearing down the Wall. I ripped away brick after shining white brick, my fingers ragged and bleeding. I wanted to stop, but my hands would not cease. I was crying as I clawed at the Wall, and when I wiped my eyes on the sleeve of my dress, I realized I was crying blood. Still, I could not fight the force that compelled me. After what seemed like years—with my fingers throbbing and my cheeks drenched in blood—the stones began to fall away on their own, and behind them was a skeleton. A child's skeleton.

"I warned her."

I started and turned to face my father. He gazed sadly at the bones in the Wall, and I stared, terrified. "Warned ... who?" I whispered.

"My daughter," he replied, still staring at the bones as though mesmerized.

"Julia?"

"No. The other one. I warned her." His face changed. Suddenly it was haggard and vicious and his eyes burned red in a blackness, like coals. "I warned her never to leave the Wall."

This time I woke screaming. My stomach was churning, my head was spinning, and I felt I might vomit. A strange sound was emanating from somewhere in the room. It took me a moment to realize it was my own sobs.

"Julia!"

I wanted to say something, but I could manage only a slight moan.

"Julia," Eytan called from what seemed like very far away. "Julia, I am coming in!"

He burst through the door to my chamber, wielding his bow and arrow. He dropped them when he saw me and rushed to my side. He touched my cheek, brushed my hair from my forehead, and ran his hands down my arms to hold my hands.

"Julia," he breathed. "Your hands."

I managed to look down and gasped. My palms were covered in blood from where my fingernails had bitten into them. Eytan stared for a moment, and it frightened me to see that he looked afraid. Then, he snatched towels from my washbasin, tore at them, and wound the strips of fabric around my injured palms. He sat down cautiously beside me, and I realized he was treating me as one would treat a spooked horse or an injured wild animal. I wondered briefly how wild I appeared. With one palm to my cheek, Eytan tipped my face up gently, until I met his gaze.

"Julia," he said softly, "it is going to be all right."

I could feel his warm breath on my face, and I remembered my tears in the dream. My hand flew to my cheek, but there was no blood there. My shoulders began to quiver, and I folded myself into Eytan's chest and wept.

* * * *

CHAPTER ELEVEN

* * * *

I awoke wrapped in Eytan's cloak, but he was nowhere to be seen. As the fog of sleep cleared, though, I thought I could hear him speaking softly somewhere not too far off. I slid out of bed and stretched. It was not until I saw my hands that the horrors of the previous night rushed back to me. Unwinding my makeshift bandages, I examined my palms. The cuts had already begun to scab over. I was anxious to find out to whom Eytan was speaking, and what he was talking about, so I tugged on the first dress my hands fell upon. I regretted it as soon as the dress settled properly on my body. It was lovely, certainly—gray velvet with gossamer sleeves—and although it was a bit large for me, it looked just as lovely on. But I did not want to be lovely. I wanted to be invisible.

I approached the door to my chamber. It was already ajar, and I worried I would be intruding on Eytan's hushed conversation in the hallway, so I waited at the door and eavesdropped. I had always been too curious for my own good.

"Please explain to me how that has anything to do with me," Eytan was saying stiffly.

"Sir, your father believes you should be present for the proceedings," a man's voice said.

"And I believe I should not be." His voice was firmer than I had ever heard it before.

"Nasich Eytan, you have been gone far too long."

Nasich?

"Your father needs you home. You must accept your duties as the heir—"

"I am well aware of my duties as heir," Eytan said, his voice louder and even harsher now. "But I have other, more vital duties at the moment, and I will not abandon them."

"You will not abandon *her.*"

Eytan was quiet for a moment. "No," he said finally. "I will not abandon her."

There was another silence, and then I heard two sets of footsteps. One echoed away, down the curving hall. The other moved toward my chamber. I turned away from the door, stunned by Eytan's words, my breath caught in my throat. What could he mean? What duty did Eytan have to *me*?

"Julia," Eytan called. "May I come in?"

"Yes," I choked out.

Eytan opened the door tentatively. I turned to him and managed a ghost of a smile, which he returned with just as much effort.

"Are you all right?" I asked him.

"I should be asking you that," Eytan replied. "But, yes. I am fine."

"Good," I said with all the confidence I could muster. "So am I."

Eytan held out his arm to me and said, "I believe it's time we found somewhere else to explore."

Linking my arm in his, I told him, "I think you are right."

Eytan was overly eager to leave the Temple of Song, but after my nightmares, I did not mind. A monk escorted us from the temple, and when we reached its main gates, Zav was waiting for us. He let out a gleeful roar and loped to me, and I thought I saw a hint of a smile flit across the stoic monk's face. I threw my arms around Zav and laid my forehead on his soft nose.

"I missed you," I whispered.

Eytan watched us with a grin, and when he led us from the temple, a weight seemed to lift off him. I was fiercely curious about the man Eytan had argued with but was too ashamed of my own nosiness to ask about it. So, for a while, we walked in silence. I never ceased to wonder at the starkness of the mountains, the shimmering snow, and the stray bird or rabbit that braved the cold. The wind whistled through the peaks, and I understood why these were called the Singing Mountains; I had never heard the world produce such music of its own accord.

I found myself lost in thought—about my mother, about all there was in the world that I did not understand. How could I have spent all my years locked within the Wall, knowing nothing but a manor, a hedge maze, the stables, and the laundry, knowing nothing of the Outside? Eytan had opened my eyes to so many things, and it suddenly occurred to me that I had no way of repaying him. My father would surely give him a generous reward if he returned me to the Wall, but Eytan had no need of more money, it seemed. And though I missed my father, the thought of returning made me shudder.

It was not until Eytan had said my name several times that I realized I was no longer moving.

"Julia," Eytan said again.

I was looking at something, I could not tell what. My mind would not register the strange sight before me. A pale figure slowly clarified in my vision, clad all in white, her dark hair streaming in the wind. Eytan's warm palm touched on my cheek, drifted hesitantly away, and then landed gently there again. Eytan forced his face into my sight line, and, finally, I came back to reality. His eyes were filled with concern and his face was tense.

Eytan brought his other hand to my face and some of the warmth returned to me. I let my eyes stray over his shoulder to where the woman had appeared. There was nothing there. Nothing but snow.

"Julia," Eytan whispered. "What did you see?"

Tears stung at my eyes. "Something is wrong," I whispered, my voice quavering. "Something is wrong. With me."

"Nightmares. Visions," Eytan said softly.

I nodded and struggled to keep my composure. I was sheltered. I was meek. But I would not fall apart. I was terrified, exhausted, and lost, but I would be strong. I put my hands on top of Eytan's and pulled them from my face. I grasped them and looked into his eyes.

"I need you to help me. I must know what is happening." My voice quavered of its own accord. "I—I'm frightened."

He pulled me into his arms, and despite my new resolve, I let him hold me as his voice filled my head with two words: "I promise."

* * ❋ * *

CHAPTER TWELVE

* * ❋ * *

"I am taking you to Saberhold," Eytan announced later that day. We had spent the morning walking in silence, stopping only for a quick meal at midday. Zav kept himself occupied chasing the rabbits, which were becoming more and more abundant as we traveled down the mountain. Kes soared above our heads. He had disappeared for a few hours, but his return seemed to break Eytan from some reverie.

His expression was hard, and I feared I had done something to upset him. But I was also weary and irritable, and I did not like feeling I was being told what to do. "Do I have a say in the matter?" I asked.

He looked wounded for a moment, but he collected himself and said, "I'm sorry. Of course you do. But there is a wise woman there who may be able to help you. She is ... well versed in these sorts of matters."

I nodded, though I was not sure the idea appealed to me.

"Besides," Eytan said lightly, "I promised you would see the knights of Saberhold. You didn't think I would forget, did you?"

I laughed. "No," I said. "I knew you would not."

We traveled east for five days, sleeping under gnarled trees, huddled in Zav's fur for warmth, eating fruit and berries and stale bread. There were no inns along this road. I was sore and hungry and constantly chilled, but I stayed cheerful, too stubborn to admit I was used to better accommodations. By the time we arrived in Saberhold, my lovely velvet dress from the temple—the monks had insisted that I keep it—was worn and muddy, and my boots were beginning to tear at their seams. I flexed my numb toes and hobbled on, wishing my blisters would go numb as well.

"Well," Eytan asked, "what do you think?"

I looked over at him, careful to keep my gaze even. "Of what?" I asked. I hoped the contempt was not apparent in my voice. I had not been taking very kindly to Eytan these past few days. It was my own fault for being so spoiled, I knew. But I could not help myself.

Eytan pointed up ahead of us. "Of Saberhold."

For a moment, I was irritated that Eytan would ask me to tip my stiff neck upwards, but once I saw the city before me, I was glad that I had looked. I gasped. I had thought the market town where Eytan and I had met had been the most stunning place I had ever witnessed. Saberhold put it to shame.

Its battlements soared into the sky, their towers so tall, their pearly roofs blended with the clouds. The entire city seemed to be one structure, its streets connected by archways that served as passages from one area of the fortress to another so the nobles that frequented them looked like they were floating over the bright streets. Some of the walls were low and roofed in wooden planks or dried hay, perfect for a smithy or a cobbler's shop. Others were tall, with turrets and flags, each fit to house a princess. The stones here were not the cold gray of the castles in my picture books. They were silver-white, like someone had splashed moonbeams upon every one of them. Flags of every color decorated the walls, boasting the crests of noble families and their knights. A place such as this must surely have been magicked into existence.

"It ... it is glorious," I said with a wistful sigh.

Eytan grinned. "I thought you would think so."

"The crests," I said, pointing at them. "Does each belong to a different knight?"

Eytan nodded and strode forward. I followed him. "All the knights of Gaerwn pledge their allegiance to Saberhold," he said. "From every city, every town, every province. I have heard it said that there is not a single noble family in Gaerwn without a knight pledged to Saberhold."

I furrowed my brow. I was a noble. Who, then, was my knight? It could not have been my father. He had been a merchant in his younger years. He had obtained several important goods for the Council, and they had lorded him for his troubles and given him my mother's hand in marriage. It was her family wealth that had become my father's holdings, her land. But it was his Wall.

I had never heard tell of a knight, though. I had never heard tell of another man in our family at all—save my mother's father, who had died long before my birth, and her brother, who had his own duchy in the south. Perhaps my uncle had a son or sons who could serve as knights to his family, but he did not visit us, and I had never met or heard of any cousins. It seemed there could be no knight in my family. And yet, when I scanned the ramparts, there it was: my family's crest. The form of a ship rippled in the wind across a blue flag dotted with tiny white gulls. Impossible.

"Eytan!" I said sharply.

Eytan looked startled. "What?"

"I have a knight!"

"What?"

I pointed up at the flag. "That is my family crest. I have a knight! Why do I have a knight? Who could he be?"

A strange look, almost like embarrassment, flitted across Eytan's face. "I don't know," he said quickly, and turned away. "Come along. You need some new clothes."

I had to jog to catch up with Eytan's quick strides. "What makes you say that?" I asked defensively, all thoughts of my knight forgotten for the moment. I felt an inexplicable need to defend my poor, tattered dress, and its even more ragged predecessor.

"If I have to see you look down at that silly frock with those forlorn eyes again, I may scream."

"I beg your pardon? My 'silly frock,' was it? And my 'forlorn eyes'?"

Eytan chuckled as he led me through the streets of Saberhold. "You thought you were being so sly, Lady Julia. But I can tell you've been moping since you snagged your sleeve on that branch four days ago. Besides, you are in desperate need of better shoes. You're limping."

"I am fine," I huffed indignantly.

"Don't be silly."

"I am not being silly, I am being perfectly sincere. If you can go without new boots and a pretty dress, then so can I."

Eytan stopped and crossed his arms in front of him. He seemed genuinely irritated now, and I had the fleeting urge to feel sorry for hassling him.

"That is more absurd still. Firstly, because I have extra clothing in my pack. Secondly, because my boots were sturdy to begin with. And thirdly, because I don't wear *dresses*." He stalked off toward a sign at the end of the street with a needle and thread painted upon it. "Silly girl," he growled as he walked.

"Bully," I countered.

He turned back to me, looking hurt. His emotions seemed to change as quickly as the clouds, and I feared I was the wind that blew them from their course. But surely we were both weary from travel and both troubled by my dreams. Perhaps we both just needed a bath and a good night's sleep. Then, we would be civil again.

Eytan composed himself, as though he had read my thoughts. "You're right. But so am I. You need clothes better suited to traveling. Fair?"

I sighed. "Fair," I conceded.

He held the door of the tailor's shop open for me. As soon as I entered, I stopped in my tracks and stared. The stone walls were hung with bolts of fabric in every color, texture, and pattern imaginable. Dresses hung off of wooden dress forms, and pin cushions and baskets of thread littered the lush carpeted floor. A plump young maiden lifted her head at our arrival, her hand pausing to hover over the stitch she was making in a pair of trousers.

"'Ello, sir. Lady," she piped. "Does the gentleman need a new cloak?"

Eytan glanced down at his rough, worn cloak. "No," he pouted. He drew himself up to his full height. "The lady needs a new dress."

The maiden nodded. "I'll call the mistress. I'm only an apprentice, ye see." She set down her work and bustled through a curtain into a back room.

"She is right, you know," I murmured. "You could use a new cloak."

Eytan rolled his eyes. "I am beginning to find you rather tedious."

I giggled. "After everything I've put you through, and only now am I tedious? I admire your patience, then."

Finally, a smile broke through Eytan's brooding. "Well, if you insist." He unclasped his cloak and threw it over a chair by the shop's stone-cut window.

Soon, a striking, middle-aged woman strode through the curtain. Her hair was piled high atop her head, and she pursed her lips at us. "Well," she said, "it would appear the two of you are in dire need of my services."

She shooed me behind a screen and instructed me to undress. As I stood in my underclothes, the woman chided Eytan for his "barbarous garb." After a short argument in which Eytan insisted his clothes were fine, and the seamstress insisted he looked as if he belonged in a cave somewhere, the seamstress forfeited, agreeing to sell him only a new cloak. She did, however, insist this one be wool, "at least."

She reminded me of the tutor my parents had brought to the Wall when I was twelve to teach me languages and sums and how to curtsy and play the harp. I had not been so well behaved back then, and the tutor only lasted two weeks before she tired of frogs in her bed and the odes I penned, addressed to her rather sizable wart.

I grinned. It was one of my happier memories from after my sister had been taken from us.

My grin fell away when the seamstress finally appeared behind the screen and surveyed me.

"Hmm," she said curtly.

I bit the inside of my cheek and wished she would not look so excited.

"Lace, I think," she murmured after a while.

My eyes widened. "Please, no lace. I beg of you."

"No, there must be some lace."

"I need something I can travel in," I insisted.

"One can travel in lace."

"It would tear," I countered. I did not add that I would feel foolish in such a garb. Eytan traveled in rough leathers. I had no need of lace and velvet on our journey, and the more I wore such frocks, the more I felt I did not belong. Perhaps, if my clothing matched our purpose, I would feel equal to it as well.

"Nonsense!" she snapped, and began to measure me. "Yes," she proclaimed finally. "I know just what to do. Come back in two days." Stepping out from behind the screen, she said to Eytan, "You." I was sure she was pointing a severe finger at him. "Wait there."

I tugged my worn dress back on and stepped out from behind the screen. Eytan was standing with his back to me, his arms crossed, staring at the workbench where the seamstress's assistant had been sitting. I smiled.

"You may look now."

Eytan turned to me. "So it's lace then, is it?"

I smirked. "Do you even know what lace looks like?"

"Of course!" He paused. "It's sort of got … you know, holes in it. Hasn't it?"

I chuckled and kicked at the hem of my dress, which was riddled with tears. "Well, if that's all it is, then it wouldn't be much of a change from what I have now."

The seamstress glided back into the room holding a cloak of deep green velvet. She tossed it to Eytan with a casual flick of her wrist.

"I suppose that will be some sort of improvement," she sighed. "Three silver pieces." She held out her hand.

Eytan made a face at her manner and placed the silver in her hand.

"I shall see you back in two days," she said, her eyes sliding over me and landing disapprovingly on my hem.

We both thanked the seamstress.

As we left, I leaned close to Eytan. "I shall repay you," I said, but he ignored me, as he had done every time I made this vow.

Zav was waiting for us outside, and Eytan patted him on the head before turning down another street.

"Boots," he declared.

I followed, hoping his curtness was simply a result of weariness and too little to eat. He had been moody ever since his encounter at the Temple of Song, and, I thought guiltily, my attitude was not helping. I was sure I was being a burden.

At the cobbler's shop, I was again awed by the richness I found inside. Dainty slippers and heavy boots sat side by side on polished wooden shelves. Tables laden with strange tools and bits of wood, leather, and fabric were scattered across the floor, beside plush chairs with cushioned footrests. I immediately felt guilty again, for I knew Eytan would pay a fortune for my nice dresses and what would surely be finely crafted shoes.

I was quite right. After the old cobbler had measured and cut and stretched and polished, he laced new traveling boots onto my feet and said, not unkindly, "That will be one gold piece, if you please."

My jaw dropped. I had never before seen a gold piece spent. Surely, my father had done so, but monetary exchanges were something else I had been sheltered from within the Wall. I assured myself, yet again, that my father would repay Eytan, but still, I felt ashamed for letting him spend so much coin on me.

Eytan, however, seemed unbothered. He placed the gold in the cobbler's open palm and shook the hand of the apprentice boy who showed us out. As Eytan pulled his hand away, I saw a flash of silver leave it.

"No need to mention it to your master," Eytan said softly.

We left the dumbstruck apprentice with his treasure and walked on.

"If I did not know any better," I said, "I would think your coin purse was enchanted."

Eytan grinned mischievously. "Perhaps it is."

We stayed at an inn that night, and I indulged in a hot bath, feeling terribly spoiled. Eytan and I ate supper together, and then he walked me to my bedroom.

"Well, goodnight," I told him.

Eytan stood, his hands behind his back, watching me intently. He opened his mouth to speak.

"Is something the matter?"

"Will you be all right?" he asked me, his voice faint. He glanced away, and I watched his jaw clench and unclench.

Something about the depth of his concern stunned me. I let my mouth hang open and stared at him, feeling the color rise in my cheeks. What was I to say? Our interactions had been strained all day; how was I to respond to such concern? I toyed briefly with the idea of slamming the door in his face but knew that would have been childish, defensive. He was only trying to help, though I still was not sure why. I was no fool. I knew Eytan was keeping things from me. But I was oddly unperturbed by this knowledge. I had the strange feeling that someday soon all would be revealed to me, and until then, despite my curiosity, at least I knew I could trust him.

Eytan's face fell as he watched me. "I am sorry about today," he said quickly. "I had ... other things on my mind. Sleep well, Lady Julia." He turned on his heel and retreated toward his own bedroom.

"Eytan!" I said before he could shut his door.

He turned. "Yes?"

I followed him down the hall, and, blushing, stood on tiptoe to kiss his cheek. I then fled to my own room and shut the door before he could recover enough to speak.

I did not sleep well. Luckily, my awakenings were not as melodramatic as they had been at the Temple of Song. *It's just as well*, I thought. Eytan could not come to my rescue every time I had a nightmare. *Let one of us have a good night's sleep.*

When I woke, the sun was just beginning to rise. I tugged on my old dress and bemoaned my ragged appearance but cheered myself by donning my new boots. Eytan and I met for breakfast, and he seemed more at ease.

"How did you sleep?" he asked me.

I paused, wondering if I should lie. "Better," I replied. It was more or less true.

"I would like to take you to the wise woman today," Eytan said carefully. He could tell I was skeptical. "I truly believe she can help you," he pressed. "She knows her trade well."

I sighed. "I shall go," I assured him. "I just ... I do not trust this sort of thing. She has some sort of ability, does she not? Something unnatural?"

"She has abilities beyond those of other people, yes," Eytan hedged.

"My last experience with magic was less than pleasurable."

Eytan sat up straighter. "What experience?"

I did not expect the urgency in his voice. I began to describe what had happened in the forest. I told Eytan of the eerie raven, the blackness, Annie's mention of the crone. I told him of my second encounter with the forest as well, when I had left him and tried to return to the Wall, although I did not want to think about it. By the time I was finished, his complexion had grown ashen.

"What is it?" I asked.

"Your situation may be graver than I feared," he murmured, more to himself than to me. He stood abruptly and took my hand. "We mustn't waste another moment. She had better be in," he added under his breath, and dragged me out of the inn onto the busy streets of Saberhold.

* * * *
CHAPTER THIRTEEN
* * * *

"Well, come *in*! Come in, my dears!" the wise woman cried. She had opened her door to us as soon as Eytan had begun to knock upon it, as if she had known we were coming. For all I knew, she *had* known. Perhaps that was one of her powers.

We followed the woman into her chambers. She was not old, nor was she young. She was very tall, beautiful in an unsettling sort of way, and she swept through the room with an otherworldly grace. There were no windows in her chambers, only layers of tapestries upon the walls and silks on every surface. Lamps and candles burned on shelves and tables.

"Oh, my Eytan, how you have grown! Why when your father, the blessed—"

"Agatha," Eytan interjected. "I would prefer if we did not speak of my father." He gave the woman called Agatha a severe look, and she searched his eyes for a moment.

"*Oh*, I see. Well, of course, love, if that's how you'd like it. Me, I think it would be better to just let the chips fall where they may, excuse the expression— you know how I love to gamble, dear."

Eytan smiled. "I know. Luckily, these chips are mine to gamble, not yours."

"Of course. Now, don't you worry about a thing, old Aggie knows what she's doing. *Well*," Agatha added, turning to me. She smiled a warm, snaggle-toothed smile, resting her hands on bony hips. I managed a smile back, but I found her rather intimidating. Her black hair matched her dress, which seemed better suited for a corpse than a living person. It was dark and layered in dreary lace, and it reminded me of the sight of my sister in her tiny funeral dress, just before Father shut her coffin and set it in the ground.

Agatha closed her mouth and gave me a sad little half-smile. "To lose your sister before you truly knew her. It is awfully sad, isn't it?" She pursed her cracked lips.

"How did you know about my sister?" I asked.

"Och, well I know everything, don't I? So long as you think it." She tapped her temple with one thin finger. Then, she sighed and, snaking her arm around my waist, led me to a chaise that sat among an assortment of desks, tables, footstools, and chests. There was no reason to the layout of the room. It almost seemed more of a storage space than a dwelling of any sort. But none of this seemed to phase Agatha.

She sat down beside me. "And by the way," she whispered, "I am much more interesting come nightfall. You will see. The two of us, we're going to spend the day together. I am going to solve the mystery of your nightmares. That I promise you."

I looked into her pale gray eyes and knew inexplicably that I could trust her.

She smiled and clapped a hand to her heart. "And how sweet of you to say so. Now, Eytan, my love, I *would* have you stay. It has been far too long. But that thought you wouldn't like me sharing is a mite distracting. Be off with you. Find yourself some employ in our lovely city, and come back at midnight for your friend. Midnight, mind you. No later."

Eytan seemed to debate for a moment, but finally, he nodded and said, "Tonight then."

He was concerned for me, I knew, so I smiled bravely. "Tonight," I replied, hoping I was right to put my trust in Agatha.

After Eytan had left Agatha's chambers, she moved from the chaise to a straight-backed chair that faced it. She had to remove from it a candelabra and the pile of old tomes it was perched on. Then she sat and studied me. "You needn't trust me, although it is lovely that you do. But you trust Eytan—more than anyone else in the world, I daresay. And if I say, it is because I *know*. And *you* know he would not leave you if he thought you were in any danger."

I smiled. "No, he wouldn't."

Agatha nodded. "Have you ever wondered why it is that you trust him so?"

I paused, twisting at the fabric of my dress. "Well, he saved my life, and he has been very kind to me."

"Does that not seem naïve to you? Do not mistake me. I mean no offense, dear. But I have seen those who would save lives just to take them in their own time."

I looked at her sharply. "Eytan is not like that."

"No," Agatha agreed. "He is not. But that makes my words no less true."

I hung my head, and frustration burned in my chest, bubbling up toward my throat. "I know," I said finally. "Ever since I left the Wall, my choices have been foolish. I have trusted those I do not know. I have traveled dangerous paths and put my life in the hands of a man I know little about. I have allowed him to care for me and pay for me, and were he a lesser man, he would surely claim that I was in his debt. Who would I be to argue after all he has done for me?

"Besides, I know he is hiding something from me, but I truly believe he has good reason for that. There is something—perhaps his past, perhaps his future—that he is running from, and he is silent on the matter. Part of me feels he is ashamed, and part of me feels he does not wish to worry me."

I huffed as the thought occurred to me. "Worry me!" I scoffed. "To think, he sees a weak girl with nightmares and hallucinations and no understanding of the world, and perhaps I am, but I can change. I shall learn and become brave and strong like he is, and like Wren is. He will see that he need not keep things from me for my own good. I *will* show him. I will ..." I trailed off, for Agatha was grinning, her eyes glistening with amusement.

"Fascinating," she said.

"How ... how did you do that?"

"Do what, my dear?"

"How did you sway me to speak in such a way? I never—"

"Never speak out? You are a well-behaved young woman, schooled in the art of silence, told that you are meant to be seen but never heard." Agatha stood and weaved gracefully through the mess of mismatched furniture. She arrived at the fireplace and hung a kettle over the flames. Holding up two teacups that had been resting on the mantle, she asked, "Tea?"

I hesitated. I reminded myself that Eytan trusted her, so I could too. "Yes, please."

Agatha blew into each cup, releasing little puffs of dust that made me cringe. She set the teacups on a small table that was, in turn, sitting atop a pile of books. From the mantle, she drew a tea tin, from which she spooned tea leaves into both of our cups.

"You have ... a beautiful home," I said hesitantly.

"Thank you, dear!" She reached for the kettle—with her bare hand, I noted, horrified—and poured our tea. Replacing the kettle, she carried our cups back to where I sat. I inspected her hands carefully, but there was not a single mark from where she had held the scalding kettle handle.

Agatha settled back in her chair and leaned in close to me. "Well, *I* hear you," she said, as if there had been no break in our earlier conversation. She straightened and continued. "And as to the other matters: you have good reason to trust Eytan, though you may not understand it yet. But even were that not the case, you are young. You are discovering. One must learn things the hard way, mustn't one? Do you think someone becomes wise by making responsible choices all the time?" Her voice dropped to a whisper. "Every once in a while we must do something impulsive.

"And yes," she continued happily, "Eytan is hiding something from you. Many things, truth be told. But nothing sinister, certainly. And he is not doing it because he thinks you need protection—although, in some ways, he is very driven to protect you. He hides things because, well, because he is not ready to accept them yet. He has quite a lot of responsibility. But, like you, he is still trying to find himself."

"I understand."

"As far as you are concerned, it is hardly your fault that you do not understand this world. The only advice I can offer you is this: keep your ears open, and your eyes peeled. See what it is that makes this world. Form your own ideas. And never be afraid to ask questions, especially of Eytan. He will not judge." Agatha took my hands in hers. "My dear, I know it is agonizing to feel that things are out of your control. There is a mystery here, and I shall try to help you solve it. But strength? Strength you must learn on your own. It blossoms within you as you become wiser. And bravery, that you already have."

"I do not feel very brave," I admitted.

"No one who is ever does."

In the hours that followed, Agatha used her gift to see into my mind. She read my palms and my cards. She threw rune stones to determine my fate. She looked through my memories as if reading a book, studying my dreams, my nightmares, and settling finally on the image of the woman in the snow.

"Do you know who she is?" I asked her.

Her eyes were closed in concentration; her hands rested on my temples. She shook her head.

"She looks familiar," I told Agatha. "As though I have seen her before, or imagined her. Or like ... like she is a part of me. She reminds me of my mother, but the features are very different, so I cannot explain why."

Agatha was silent.

"I feel as though she is trying to tell me something. There is an urgency in her, like she is pleading with me. But I cannot say what it is she needs. I cannot help her. I do not even know her name."

Agatha let out a long breath. "There is power in her. I cannot tell from whence it comes. She and the dreams are connected; this you know. And the encounter with the raven, that must mean something as well. But your mind, child, is a deep and complex place. It is a labyrinth in the dark, and I cannot find my way through."

"What does that mean?"

"It does not bode well. It tells me that there is something in you we have yet to see. Something powerful. Perhaps something dangerous."

I drew away from her. "I am not dangerous."

"No, child. But there is something. Perhaps it is following you, feeding off of you. Or perhaps it is within you. And it is something I do not know how to explain. The closest I can come is to compare it to a curse. But it is embedded much deeper in you than any curse I have ever seen."

"Can I break this curse?"

Agatha sighed. "In your fortune, I have read future struggles. A long journey, a hunger, fear."

I snorted. "Are you sure you were not reading my past?"

"No, this is something darker. I see sand, and burning sun, and a pit so dark and deep that you may never find your way out. One thing is certain: you will go to Oro. There will be help for you there. But after that, there will be much hardship." She took my hands in hers again. "Whatever I am encountering in your mind, it is keeping me from seeing a resolution, but I can tell you this: follow a moon, a beetle, and a vial. Ride the winds to the heart of a lie. These things will help you find your way." Agatha dropped my hands, sagged in her chair, and her eyes rolled back in her head until only the whites were showing.

I gasped. "Are you ...?"

She began to tremble. "It is midnight. The hour is upon you to leave. Heed my words."

"But it does not make any *sense*!"

"Go!"

But before I could move, Agatha's face began to change. Her skin grew softer, her lips fuller. The whites of her eyes turned to black, and she gave me a grin full of malice, beautiful and terrifying at the same time. She reached a slender arm, once bony and dry, toward me, and her skin shone pearly white. Her tapered fingers grasped at me, and she pulled me toward her with a strength I had never encountered. She licked her lips with a quick tongue, and her splendor took my breath away, and with it, my will to fight. She gathered me in her arms, buried her face in my neck, and groaned.

"So sweet," she whimpered. Her hands explored my waist. "That power ... let me taste it, child." Her lips brushed my skin, and somewhere deep inside me, revulsion stirred. But the power in her was calling to me, and I was content to give in, pushing all my doubts aside.

I shuddered and leaned into her. My limbs went slack, and only her embrace held me upright. She was much taller than I; my feet trailed on the ground as she drew herself up to her full height, lifting me with her. Vaguely, I heard shouting from outside, but I was drifting into a deep peacefulness, punctuated by surges of some pleasant sensation for which I had no name. I felt Agatha's power surrounding us, pressing us together and pressing outward at the same time. Someone was *screaming*. But Agatha's power held a fragrance so delicious I could taste it, and I shivered in ecstasy as she grasped the back of my neck with one hand.

"Julia!" I was momentarily intrigued by the paradox of sound growing clearer as I drifted further from reality. "*Julia!*" My eyes fluttered, closed, and my sigh caught in the back of my throat. "Julia, fight!"

My eyes snapped open as the voice permeated the fog surrounding my mind. Eytan. I blinked. Something was flowing from my mouth, my eyes, my hands. It felt like blood, but cooler, thinner. I slid my eyes to the side and watched a shimmering mist drift from my fingers, like gossamer threads, purple and silver. I tasted the same mist as it left my mouth and streamed down my cheeks. It was surrounding Agatha's body, and she jerked as she fed on it.

From somewhere dark and very far away, Eytan roared, "Julia!"

My heart thudded an uneven rhythm, and I tried to gasp. I could not breathe. I lifted my hands and pressed them between my body and Agatha's. I ripped her soft hand from my neck and threw myself to the ground, out of her grasp. The rush of power and the flow of my mist-blood ceased abruptly with a sharp *crack*, and Agatha too fell.

The thud of a door slammed into flagstones sent a jolt of pain through my spinning head. Eytan was before me, his bow drawn, an arrow pointed at Agatha's throat.

Agatha looked up at him, her lips parted. "Please," she beseeched. "I *need* her."

"Julia, can you stand?" Eytan asked without turning to me.

I pushed myself off the floor and tugged myself up, using Eytan's belt as an anchor.

"Stay behind me," Eytan instructed.

I put my hands on his shoulders, too dazed to respond and too weak to stand without his support.

"No! No, do not take her. Let her stay with me, Eytan. I shall treat her like a princess."

"I'm sorry," Eytan said, his voice soft and rough all at once. "I tried to get back sooner. Agatha, I'm so sorry." He began backing towards the exit, leading me with him, his arrow still trained on Agatha.

"*Eytan!*" Agatha cried. She lurched forward, crawling after us, but we were over the threshold, and when she reached it, she was stayed by some invisible barrier. "No!" she shrieked as she recoiled. "*No!*" Her screams echoed through the streets as Eytan kicked Agatha out of the way and pulled the door shut behind us.

Finally, he lowered his bow. He turned to me, careful to hold me upright as he took away the support of his shoulders. I swayed on my feet. My mouth felt dry, my eyes too wide for my skull. I was suddenly very cold—a cold that radiated from the inside out, a deeper, harsher cold than I had felt even in the mountains.

I met Eytan's eyes and my entire body began to shake. "Help me," I whispered. Then, my world went black.

* ✳ ✳ ✳ *

CHAPTER FOURTEEN

* ✳ ✳ ✳ *

I drifted in and out of consciousness for what seemed like days, and my vision swam with nightmarish images, occasionally relieved by Eytan's strained visage. I felt weak, and no matter how many blankets Eytan heaped upon me, I shivered uncontrollably.

When I finally came back to my senses, I was in a small room with a thatched roof and white walls. It was day, and the light shining through the windows hurt my eyes. I groaned, and before I could blink, Eytan was at my side.

"Hello," I murmured.

He smiled and brushed my hair from my forehead. "Hello."

"Where are we?"

"At the Phoenix Inn, just outside of Saberhold. It is safe here."

I tried to roll to one side and sit up, but my head spun, and I sank back into my pillows. Eytan leaned over me in concern. It took a moment for the spots to clear from my vision. My eyes throbbed.

"What happened?"

Eytan kept his hand on my forehead. "It's my fault. I knew Agatha could endanger you if I did not return in time. I ... I was delayed. I am so sorry, Julia."

I winced. "It is not your fault." My cheeks flushed. "Why am I so helpless?"

Eytan furrowed his brow. "Helpless? Julia, I have never known anyone who could escape the grasp of someone like Agatha. What you did, it was incredible."

My head swam. "She is not human, is she?"

"No, not entirely. You were in no danger, so long as you left by midnight." He stood abruptly, his shoulders tensed, and he slammed one hand onto the doorframe. "I should never have left you there with her alone. I should have stayed, made certain you were safe, made *sure*—"

"Eytan," I said softly.

He turned to me, his jaw tight.

I beckoned, and he returned to his seat beside me on the bed. "You mustn't blame yourself. I am safe, and relatively well, I think. And you saved me. Again. Besides, Agatha did help me, before ..." I shivered.

"Help you?"

I closed my eyes, trying to remember. "She said ... to follow the moon, and a beetle, and a vial. She spoke of sand and a dark pit and of following the wind to the heart of ... of a lie. And she said we should go to Oro. There is so much I do not understand, but it is clear where our journey should take us next."

Eytan nodded. "The swordsmiths."

"Eytan?"

"Yes?"

"How long have I been ... indisposed?"

Eytan paused, his face pained. "Two months."

My heart leaped to my throat and I bolted upright. "Two *months*?" I regretted moving as soon as I had done it. My chest suddenly burned, my head pounded fiercely, my vision blurred. I reached out for Eytan to steady myself and gripped his vest.

He put an arm around my shoulders. "You must not strain yourself."

I gasped and leaned tentatively towards him, resting my forehead on his chest. The sound of his heartbeat steadied me and eased the pain in my head.

"How can that be?" I whispered.

Eytan stroked my hair. "What Agatha inflicted on you was powerful magic.

She meant to devour your soul. You would have been made a thrall, an empty vessel capable only of sensation. None have ever escaped such an attack before. You were weakened, feverish. It was all I could do to get you to eat." He was silent for a moment, and then, so softly I could barely hear him, he rasped, "I feared you would not survive."

I did not feel as though I had been asleep for two months, but I certainly looked it. I yelped when I saw my reflection, insisted on a bath, and dressed quickly in one of the three garments the seamstress in Saberhold had prepared for me weeks ago.

"She was not pleased with me when I told her you could not come for a fitting," Eytan said sheepishly as he showed me the dresses. "She kept muttering about final alterations."

I smiled, retreated behind my dressing screen, and traded in my nightgown for a simple purple frock trimmed in silver lace. My body was slow and clumsy, my limbs heavy. Every movement was an effort. I had not been slim before my ordeal. I had inherited my father's stocky build, not my mother's lean frame. But I had lost much of my weight, lying in bed so long. The dress was too large for me. I resolved to eat heartily until I could fill it out once more.

I emerged and held my arms out. "Well," I asked Eytan, "what do you think?"

He smiled. "Beautiful."

I blushed and ran my hand down my side. "And to think I doubted her about the lace."

Eytan shrugged. "I meant you," he admitted offhandedly, "but I suppose the dress is nice as well."

My blush deepened, but he was fiddling with his bow and quiver and did not see.

I was eager to make up for lost time, but I was very weak. We spent another fortnight at the Phoenix Inn while I gathered my strength. At first, I could eat little more than porridge, but once my body reacclimated to heavier foods, I ate with a fervor that made Eytan laugh.

Eytan helped me recover by stretching my limbs and encouraging me to press against his palms with my hands and feet. He tied parcels of small stones to my arms and legs and made me lift them. He took me on walks around the grounds, first short ones, leaning upon Zav for support, then longer outings, until finally, I snapped the makeshift walking stick I had needed in two and proclaimed, "My gown is made of lace. I am *not*."

Eytan relented, and we packed our things.

"Zav, we're going!" I called, practically dancing into the stables. I kissed him right between his molten gold eyes and he let out a gleeful rumble.

As we left the stables, the sun glinted off of something moving too swiftly to pinpoint. Eytan lifted an arm and Kes alighted on his sleeve, clicking his beak and nibbling gently on Eytan's ear.

"Where has he been?" I asked.

"I had a missive to send to my father."

"In Bahir?"

Eytan nodded.

I sensed, as I often did with Eytan, that the words he left unsaid were glinting in his eyes, but I made no mention of it. His privacy was the least I could give him after all he had done for me.

From the border of Phoenix Town, we could see the gates of Saberhold. I took one last look at my family crest as we passed by the mighty city, and stroked Zav's coat to steady my nerves.

Oro was on the northernmost border of Gaerwn, near rainy, rocky shores where ancient ports had received iron and strange metals from across the seas. Eytan decided we should head west first, and travel north upon the shore, an easier route with soft ocean breezes to help restore my strength. I was delighted. This route would take us back through the Firthen Forest, where I had no doubt

Wren and her band of outlaws would welcome us with open arms.

Eytan smiled at my excitement and said, "Yes. I am eager to see Wren once more. There is much that weighs on my mind lately."

I hesitated. "Things you cannot tell me?"

Eytan thought for a moment and replied, "Things I am not yet ready to tell you. I will," he added. "I swear to you, I will."

I frowned, but not at his words so much as at the feeling that had stirred within me. I did not feel lied to. I did not feel as if secrets were being kept from me. I felt ... sad for him. I wanted to embrace him and tell him everything would be all right. But instead, I simply told him, "I trust you."

The outlaws were indeed happy to see us, but to my disappointment, Wren was not among them. She had left on some errand. Still, the outlaws had happy tidings of the refugees we had aided months before. They were helping the people establish a new village on the outskirts of the forest, and all seemed well. We had our fireside revelries as before, and I requested my favorite songs of the outlaws before I turned in for sleep.

I lay curled up against Zav's stomach, listening to a soft wind whisper through the trees, but sleep would not come. I had slumbered for two months, and now I wanted to be awake. I wanted to live. I wanted to solve the mysteries that surrounded me. But more than all of that, I wanted very much to sort out my feelings for Eytan. At times, I thought I felt something between us, but he could be so vexing.

Careful not to wake Zav, I crawled out into the night, then made my way to Eytan's tent. There was a light glowing within. I hung back.

"I do not know what is right any longer," I heard Eytan murmur.

"I understand." It was Wren's voice, I was sure. I had not heard or seen her return. A surge of feelings for her rose in my chest, and I felt more confused than ever.

"I feel I am torn in two," Eytan was saying, as if he could read my mind. "There is the part of me that wants only to aid her, and then there is my responsibility to my father."

"But you don't even want that responsibility."

Eytan paused. "That is what I thought as well. But Julia has taught me much about myself during our time together. We are very much the same, the two of us. Both running from our homes, both looking for ourselves. But I think ... Wren, is it possible to find yourself in another? Even before she knew it, I think part of me belonged to her. And now ... now I feel I must do what is right. After I help Julia, I must return to my father."

"What will that mean for her?"

"She does not understand my feelings. If she knew what I had done ..." There was another silence, and then Eytan let out a pained sigh. "I do not know."

I returned to my tent before Wren or Eytan could discover me and spent the remainder of the night pondering Eytan's words. When I finally drifted off to sleep, the nightmares were there to meet me.

In the morning, Eytan ate swiftly and then informed me that we should be on our way. "We have a lot of distance to cover," he said, "and the sooner we discover what is causing your dreams, the better."

Disappointed at being ushered from Firth so soon and incensed by the night's eavesdropping, I snapped, "Are you that eager to be rid of me?"

Eytan looked stricken, and I felt instantly guilty. "No," he stammered. "Of course not."

After my outburst, our farewells with the outlaws were strained. Wren wished us a safe journey and, after embracing Eytan, she kissed me on the cheek.

"Lady Julia," she whispered. "Eytan has a weight on his shoulders you cannot imagine, but he *does* care for you, and he is trying."

I bit my lip. "I understand," I told her. "And what of you?"

Wren gave me a roguish smile that made my heart flutter. "Oh, make no mistake. I care for you too. But I can see where your heart lies."

"Really? Because I certainly cannot."

She kissed my cheek again, but this time her lips lingered near my ear. "If your heart tells you to return, you know just where to find me. But if it tells you something different ... well, I am grateful for our time together, and I will always be a friend."

The outlaws were milling about, and Eytan was watching, but I could not help myself. I turned my head and brushed her lips with my own, just for a moment. "You are incredible," I told her. "Did you know that?"

"Trust me," she said, grinning hugely, "I know."

"Thank you. For everything." I squeezed her hand once more and turned towards Eytan, whose gaze was cast downward as he kicked at a pebble, seemingly with intense interest.

Eytan and I began our trek to Oro in silence, until finally the tension overwhelmed me and I said, "This is ridiculous."

Eytan raised an eyebrow. "What is?"

"I told you I was resigned to the secrets, but clearly I am not. What I said to you in Firth was unfair. I am sorry. I do not need to know everything, but ..."

"Yes. I know." He paused, struggling to find the right words. "I ... my father is an important man in Bahir. *Very* important. And the time is almost upon me to take over his position. I have spent most of my life gallivanting across the world, looking for adventure, and rebelling against my father in every way possible. But my time with you has made me understand what it means to have responsibilities. After all of this is over, I will return home and take my place in the family."

"And what of"—*us*, I thought—"our friendship?"

Eytan stared at his feet. "In truth, I am not sure."

I nodded, and we walked on. This was not how I had envisioned the world outside the Wall to be.

* * * * *
CHAPTER FIFTEEN
* * * * *

Oro was old—little more than ruins, nestled in mist and a light snowfall on the side of a cliff, and it seemed as though the entire city had been painted over in silvers and grays. Still, it was beautiful, in a sad sort of way, and I was immediately drawn to it.

It reminded me of a story my mother had told me once, about a woman who was trapped in a castle for hundreds of years. As the seasons passed, the castle became decrepit, and nothing grew there, save the white rose bushes that barred the gates and drawbridge. Men would come for her, having heard tell of her beauty, and would seek her hand in marriage, but she would have nothing of chivalry or love. She wanted only her castle and her roses. She was not trapped after all; she was content. She did not age or change in the least, and she did not leave the dying castle.

One day, a merchant man was passing by the castle, and his horse was startled by a wolf's howl. The horse bucked the merchant off and galloped away into the forest. The man was injured, and the woman watched from her tower as wolves congregated, drawn by the scent of his blood. She left the castle for the first time in three hundred years in order to save the man, and as she exited, the rose bushes coiled in on themselves to make way for her. She fought off the wolves long enough to help the man inside. She tended to his wounds, and, eventually, they fell in love. After a time, they left the castle together. The moment the woman was outside of its walls, it collapsed in on itself, leaving only the ghosts of so many years of solitude and blocks of crumbled stone.

As a child, I had dreamed that one day the Wall would crumble like that so I could have my freedom. Looking at Oro, at the city of ruins, I wondered if my absence could have destroyed the Wall, like the woman in the story had destroyed her castle.

Eytan led me into Oro, over a path of flagstones that shook under Zav's heavy steps. Past the columns of what might once have been a temple, there was a smithy, erected from ancient stones and bits of wood and straw. There was no one visible within, but its fires burned.

"Hello?" Eytan called. "Hello? Is anyone here?"

A head of shaggy, jet black hair appeared from behind a vat of water, and a similar head popped out from around the side of the smithy. "Hullo," said the first man. As he stood, I could see his face properly. He was young, smiling, and soot-covered.

"Greetings," said the second, walking out to the front of the structure. It took me a moment to realize that the speaker was not a man at all. She was a tall, lean woman with hair that stopped at her jaw and features so like the man's that they must have been twins.

"Have you come for a sword?" the brother asked.

"I know you, don't I?" said the sister, pointing at Eytan.

"I was here once, many years ago, when a blade was forged for my father. I don't remember the two of you—"

"Oh, we were much younger then," the brother said. "And much prettier. I'm Malek, and this is my sister, Maeve."

"Yes, I'm Maeve," the sister added. She leaned toward me and winked. "And I'm still pretty."

I laughed.

Eytan shifted uncomfortably and said, "I *have* come for a sword, in fact.

And the lady will be needing one as well."

My eyes grew wide. "*Me*? What would I possibly do with a sword?"

"She's right," mused Maeve. She pointed to Eytan. "*You* need a sword."

"But *she* needs daggers," Malek finished. "Two of them. Thin. Light. Long, I think. Something sleek and efficient." He and his sister turned and walked into the smithy, beckoning for Eytan and me to follow.

"Dangerous but elegant," Maeve was saying as she poked around at various metal tools on the shelves of the forge.

"Swords are elegant," Eytan muttered. He leaned against the doorframe, looking petulant. I laughed behind my hand.

"Yes, yes, you'll have a sword," Malek assured Eytan, reaching out to take the bellows his sister was holding out to him.

"And you will have daggers," Maeve told me. "They will be works of art, my lady, the likes of which you've never seen before."

"I am sure they would be," I said. "But I really have no need for weapons."

Maeve's face grew serious. "Need you have aplenty, my lady," she said quietly. "Trust us. My brother and I, we understand the way of it. Need you have." Her face brightened again, and she beckoned for us to stand beside her. "Come along, then. This won't take but a moment."

Malek and Maeve stood facing each other across a huge slab of stone. There was a large fire burning at its head and a series of stone basins at the opposite end. The slab was carved with runes I could not read.

"The sword first, I think," said Malek as he worked the bellows to stoke the fire.

"Yes, most definitely," Maeve agreed.

The siblings thrust their hands out over the stone and looked at Eytan.

"Think about your sword," Malek instructed.

"What do you mean?" Eytan asked, eyeing them warily.

Maeve sighed. "Somewhere inside you is *your sword*, the sword that was meant to be wielded by you and only you. You probably should have come and claimed it sooner, but no matter. Just think of the sword that will do your works, and we shall create it."

"How?" I asked.

Maeve smiled broadly. "Watch and see."

Eytan closed his eyes, and I wondered what imaginings raced through his head. Would he think of chivalry? Of honor and nobility? Or would he think of blood and violence and the battle cry?

Malek and Maeve searched Eytan's face carefully, nodded to one another, and clasped each other's forearms over the table, their arms crossed at the wrists. They breathed in tandem, and their linked arms traversed the length of the stone, leaving thick, shimmering, hot air in their wake. Suddenly, molten liquid began to stream across the slab, slipping into the engravings of the runes. When they released each other, something shifted, like a shadow flitting past too quickly for the eye to see, and then the air settled once more. Where moments ago there had been only stone, a gleaming sword now lay. It was long and slender, its handle curved like the wing of a swan, its tip so sharp it glinted in the murky light.

I gasped, and Eytan stared in bewilderment.

"Well," Malek prompted.

"Take it," urged Maeve.

Eytan walked slowly to his sword. When his hand closed around its hilt, the weapon seemed to hum. He lifted it from the stone, and the blade sang, sweeping its way through the air with a grace I did not know steel could possess.

Maeve handed Eytan a sheath, grinning proudly.

"It is beautiful," I whispered.

"It is at that." Eytan met both twins' gazes in turn. "Thank you."

Malek and Maeve swept into matching bows, then turned to me.

"And now," Maeve crowed.

"For the lady." Malek inclined his head to me. "Imagine your blades, lady."

How could I imagine a weapon that I did not know how to wield? I furrowed my brow and closed my eyes, sighing in exasperation. My blades ... they would have to be small and light, with slender hilts that could fit easily at my waist or in a sheath in my boots. Blades that would do my works. Simple, then, and sharp. As pure as moonlight, as true as the stars. Yes. Those would be my blades. I opened my eyes.

Before me, glistening on the slab, were two narrow daggers with clear, multi-faceted handles—handles made from pure crystal. I took one in each hand, and they began to glow with the soft milky shimmer of the moon. Warmth spread through my hands and up my arms, and it was as though the blades were a part of me. I could feel my heartbeat pulse through their hilts.

"I ... I don't know what to say."

The siblings grinned. "They are fitting," Maeve said.

"Yes," I agreed quickly. "Now, if only I knew how to use them."

Maeve may have been a gleeful sort—reminding me a bit of a jet black hunting dog we'd had when I was young, whom my father had been forced to relegate to the house, for he was too jubilant and playful to focus on the hunt—yet, with a weapon in her hand, she was an entirely different creature. She handled her own sword with a grace and precision I had never thought possible. She and Eytan sparred as though dancing, and the ruins of Oro echoed with the music of their clashing blades.

Malek and I sat watching nearby.

"Do you spar?" I asked him.

"Oh, a bit. I can hold my own in a fight, but I'm more interested in the smithing. And gardening. Remind me to show you my herbs."

I smiled. "Your sister is ..." I had no words for her skill. "Exquisite," I said finally. "An exquisite fighter."

"Best swordswoman that ever lived, if you ask me," Malek said, his arms crossed casually across his chest. "Best swords*man*, for that matter, as well. Of course, as her brother, I may be biased." He leaned toward me. "And don't tell her I've said so."

"For you, it'll be different," Maeve called to me without a hint of effort in her voice as she countered one of Eytan's blows and dodged the next. "Your

daggers can fend off the steel of any blade, but you'll need a different form."
She glided away from Eytan and sprang back so quickly, I thought perhaps I
had imagined the movement. And then her blade was at Eytan's throat.

Eytan surrendered happily. "Incredible," he said.

"That was rather standard technique for swordplay," Maeve told me as she
bowed to Eytan. "So now you know what sorts of moves you've got to counter." She held out her hand to me.

"I couldn't possibly!" I said.

"Do not fear. We will begin easily enough."

For the remainder of that day, and the next, and for many days after, Malek
and Maeve taught me the ways of swordplay. First, posture and movement,
like dancing, yet somehow infinitely more graceful. They taught me proper
stance and proper grip. Each lesson was steeped in detail and concentration. It
was a fortnight before I raised my blades against them at all. By that time, my
body had fully recovered from my long sleep. My clothes no longer hung loose,
and my muscles were stronger than they had ever been before. Finally, Maeve
showed me how to strike and how to counter, how to catch a sword between my
two daggers and deflect its blow. I had no great skill, but my daggers felt right
in my hands. For the first time in my life, I felt capable of taking care of myself.

My lessons left me so weary that I was rarely visited by the nightmares I had
grown to dread. The relief of undisturbed sleep drove me to study all the more,
and Malek and Maeve were more than happy to oblige.

It was not only sword fighting that they taught me. Malek did indeed show
me his herb garden, which surpassed my wildest imaginings.

We were walking together, sipping from skins of water, as Malek told me
silly stories of his and Maeve's childhood. The stories seemed queer somehow,
with details that felt out of place, or references to people and places that I was
sure I had read of only in history books. Yet, each time I ventured a question,
Malek just laughed me off and said, "No matter!"

Then, suddenly, we were at a sheer drop. A lower level of the ancient city
was laid out before us, and we viewed it from the top of a flagstone wall. Most

of the structures below us had long since crumbled, but there was a vast stone enclosure backing up to the wall we stood atop. The other three sides were flanked by low walls, one of which had a great stone archway in its center. It might once have been a city square. In the middle of the square was a stone fountain filled with murky water and some sort of beautiful floating flowers. Spiraling out from the fountain were green plots, dotted here and there with tiny flowers in shades of white, yellow, and purple.

"*This* is your herb garden?"

Malek swelled with pride. "Do you like it?"

"Absolutely!"

"I had hoped you would say so." He led me to a stairway hewn into the side of the wall and down into the garden. He knelt by a bush nestled against the high wall and plucked a yellow-and-white flower.

I took it from his outstretched hand and smelled it. "Honeysuckle," I said.

"Helps with headaches and fevers."

"I didn't know."

"Useful things, plants," Malek said. "Lovely, yes, and some of them are quite good for cooking. But they do so much more than that." He pointed to a row of squat, green-leafed plants. "Mint," he continued. "Good for the stomach." He pointed again. "Rosemary clears the nose. And that one there, with the small white blossoms with the yellow centers? Chamomile. It helps wounds heal." He glanced at me then, a knowing look in his eyes. "Brewed into a tea, it can soothe one's sleep as well."

"That's ... something I shall keep in mind," I murmured.

"Of course, not all of my plants are innocuous." He led me down one of the many spiral pathways to a section of the garden that was secluded in great cast-iron cages. "Take care not to touch," he added softly, almost fearfully.

A chill crept over me. "Why? What are these?"

He indicated a lush, bushy plant with large, vibrant green leaves and tiny white flowers that looked almost to be made of lace. "It is called hemlock. The leaves and flowers are dangerous, but the roots are deadly. If consumed, they clutch the unlucky soul's stomach in an iron grip until the victim succumbs to death."

I stared at him, my mouth open, and said nothing.

"And this," he motioned now to a shrub with dull green leaves and berries shiny and black, so enticing that a sick part of me wanted to reach through the bars of the cage and pop one into my mouth, despite Malek's cautions.

"What is it?" I asked in a hushed voice. The feeling of telling ghost stories overtook me again.

"Deadly nightshade. It will stop the heart if eaten."

"Stop the ..." I spun towards him. "Why would you *have* these?"

Malek chuckled. "Do not fear, Lady Julia. I am no murderer. I would never wish that sort of death on anyone. Why do you think I've caged them as I have? No, they are not to be used." He paused and stared at the lovely, deadly plants with a sort of wonder. "They are a reminder."

"A reminder of what?"

"That there is darkness in the world, as immutably, as naturally as there is light. That not all that seems innocent is safe." He glanced at me. "That something should not be underestimated simply because it has beauty." He shrugged. "I thought it a lesson you might wish to learn."

I pondered for a moment. Was he calling me naïve? Or was he suggesting that I, too, had a strength that lay beneath the surface? Perhaps it was both.

From that day on, I spent much of my days with my daggers in hand, but I also visited the herb garden with Malek, tending to his "green children," as he called them. It was a funny balance, I thought, learning the arts of war and cultivation side by side. And learn I did. I learned to pare and prune, to identify plants by smell, by touch, and by taste (when it was safe). I learned which plants soothed aches and pains, which cleared rashes, which could be brewed into teas or soaked into rags and placed on sore muscles, which could be made into tinctures by soaking them in alcohol or vinegar for weeks at a time.

He taught me which types of soil were best for certain plants, how much sunlight and water they required, which climates suited them best. The more he explained, the more puzzled I became. The plants seemed to be from a dozen different regions, some native to Gaerwn, others brought across the seas by traders. They were native to different climes and required vastly different care from one another. How could he keep them all thriving together in one small garden?

When I asked Malek the question directly, he merely laughed and said, "A good gardener is capable of extraordinary things, my lady."

I smirked. Let Eytan keep his secrets, I thought. I was growing accustomed to them, and as I had reminded myself many a time when speaking with Eytan, I too had things I kept to myself.

The twins had proven their magic the first day we met them, when they had made us our miraculous weapons. But I suspected their powers went beyond even that. They seemed to know things they could not know, much as Agatha had that day back in Saberhold. I tried not to be afraid, for they had been nothing but kind. Yet, it seemed to me that there was no magic in the world without some darkness to it.

Eytan and I practiced our combat for hours each day and spent our remaining time aiding Malek and Maeve with chores around their smithy, the herb garden, and the small cottage they had welcomed us into. I explored the ruins, finding strange carvings on crumbling slabs and columns. The twins claimed ignorance of the indecipherable language I found upon the stones, but I was not sure I believed them. I copied the inscriptions into a journal, determined to research their meanings. Eytan, meanwhile, wrote letter after letter. He stayed up late into the night, writing by candlelight and burning draft after draft of his missives in the flames.

One clear day, as he was helping me practice archery with his beautifully carved bow, I turned to him, our faces close enough that they almost touched.

"You need to return to Bahir, don't you?"

"I—what makes you say ...?"

I laughed and stepped away from him. He relaxed immediately. "I know you have been lingering here because you don't wish to return. Malek and Maeve have taught me much. Enough for me to protect myself. And Agatha—" He flinched at the mention of her name; I too had to steel myself to utter it, but though I feared her still, I no longer blamed her for what had transpired. I pressed on. "Agatha foretold sand and the burning sun—"

"That could be anywhere."

"Don't interrupt," I chided, and Eytan sulked a bit, only making me laugh again. I took his hand and softened my tone. "We both know where we are meant to go."

"We?" For a moment, Eytan looked like a child, hope shining in his eyes.

"Well yes, of course. It was *my* future Agatha read. Surely that means I must go with you."

* * * * *
CHAPTER SIXTEEN
* * * * *

I wished dearly for Malek and Maeve to accompany us to Bahir. We had become very close in our weeks together, and now I could not imagine leaving them behind. But their lives were bound to Oro. I could not explain how I knew it, but it was there, a knowledge I could not place. And so we bid them farewell. Even Zav tried to herd them along with us as Eytan and I set off. I called him to my side, and we departed, leaving our hosts behind in the mists. Soon I could no longer see them, or the ruins of Oro. It was as if the whole cliffside had disappeared into the clouds.

We made our way to a port city not far south. There, a ship awaited us—a product of one of Eytan's letters, I was sure. It would be a month before we reached the shores of Midbar; Eytan had told me that soon after we met. It seemed a lifetime ago now.

I had never seen a real ship before. My father had kept small replicas, encased in glass bottles, in his study. He said they reminded him of his days as a merchant, but that was a life I could never imagine for him. I knew only the father who existed within the Wall, trapped there like I was, trapped like the ships in his bottles.

True ships were incomprehensibly vast, with none of the stillness of their bottled counterparts. The ship that awaited us was of dark, intricately carved wood, its white sails so crisp and pure against the azure sky that it almost hurt my eyes to look upon them. The crew were all dark-skinned. Some were naturally so, like Eytan, and others were clearly from Gaerwn, but with skin turned leathery-brown from the sun. Every one of them had muscles like a blacksmith, or like the strongman from the circus that had visited us within the Wall when I was young. I heard several different languages being shouted at once as various sailors called to each other. Some of the tongues I recognized, though I could not understand the words. Others were so new to me that they sounded more like music than words. I wanted to learn them all.

The captain greeted us at the gangplank, immediately sweeping into a low bow, her fist pressed against her chest. She was a short, slender woman dressed in black trousers, a black tunic, a black leather vest, and a black greatcoat outfitted with shining brass buttons. Her skin was the same shade as Eytan's. The only indications of her age were the lines around her striking green eyes, and her hair, which was of pure silver, braided intricately, twining from beneath her hat and falling over her shoulder as she bowed. Her braid was so long that it brushed against her sword belt, and it was wound through with strips of leather and something deep green and lacy that, had I not known better, I might have identified as seaweed. Despite her slight frame, she was somehow the most commanding presence I had ever encountered.

"We are honored to have you sail with us, Nasich," the captain said. She spoke the tongue of Gaerwn with a beautiful accent that somehow reminded me of the waves that lapped at her ship.

There was that word again, I thought. *Nasich.*

Eytan bowed in return and said something to her in Midbari. It was a lovely language, throaty and melodic. Zav's ears perked up at the sound, and I wondered if he recalled the language of the Lion Boy.

The captain conversed easily to Eytan in what I assumed was also her native tongue, and then she turned to me and bowed again. "Lady Julia," she said in the Gaerwn tongue, "I am, humbly yours, Captain Vered of Bahir, and this, my ship, is the *Aliyah.* Your companion's father I have known for many years, since Eytan was but a small thing, and I was already sailing these blessed seas. I am honored to provide you with passage to Midbar. Please tell me of any wishes you may have so that I may make your journey very comfortable."

I curtsied low, hoping she would attribute my red cheeks to the cold wind. I was embarrassed by her formality. Yes, I was a noble, but I was no one of consequence. I didn't deserve such reverence, especially from one as impressive as Captain Vered. "I am obliged," I told her in my most lady-like voice. "And I look forward to journeying upon your grand vessel." Perhaps the manners lessons upon which my father had long ago insisted were not entirely for naught.

As soon as I set foot aboard the *Aliyah*, I felt giddy with excitement, but also with fear. My feet did not wish to stay beneath me; my stomach felt the same as it had when I had fallen out of a tree as a child, like it was about to tumble right out of my body.

"I feel I'm going to be ill," I told Eytan.

"You'll grow used to it," he assured me. "Perhaps my surprise will make you feel better."

"Surprise?"

He took my hand and led me belowdecks. Zav padded after us, looking as unsteady as I felt. Eytan and I moved to flank him, our hands on his muscular shoulders, guiding him. He moaned softly, a sound that said both "thank you" and "how could you do this to me?" all at once. I giggled and planted a kiss on his furry head.

We took Zav to the hold first. I wanted him to stay with me, but the cabins were not large enough for him to move about comfortably, Eytan explained. The crew had made him a stable in the hold, stocked with hay, blankets, and a pen nearby filled with livestock, which were to be fed to him throughout the journey, since meat already butchered would rot, and salted meat was harmful to a lion's constitution. The crew clearly knew how to care for him, I thought in relief.

I ruffled his mane and kissed him between the eyes, his favorite show of affection. "I'll check on you often," I promised. "Be good."

Zav gave another low rumble and looked up at me, his molten eyes beseeching.

"You'll be all right," Eytan said, patting him on the rump. "And you'll eat like a king!"

Zav harrumphed, and with one last kiss, I left him to sulk.

Eytan then led me down the hall and into a small cabin with a bed, a wash-basin, and dozens of beautiful books.

"This is your cabin," he told me.

"Mine?" I ran my fingers along the leather-bound volumes. Their rich smell permeated the room, gentler than the sharp, salty air above. "Truly?"

Eytan was grinning nearly as widely as I was. "I sent for them. There are histories, legends, and dictionaries of a myriad of languages. I thought you'd like to try your hand at interpreting those letters you were scribbling down in Oro."

I flung my arms around his neck without a second's hesitation. Books had long been my escape, my only portal to the outside world. They had taught me of things the Wall never could. I had not realized until this moment how dearly I had missed them.

"I love it," I said into Eytan's ear. "Thank you." I kissed him on the cheek. "Thank you!"

He was blushing. "You're most welcome."

I was less thankful to Eytan in the days that followed. The seas were quite calm, if his claim could be believed, but I felt horribly ill all the same. I could barely keep down any food, palatable though it was, and I dared not go above deck for the first week. I stayed in my cabin as often as possible, for even moving about the room made me feel nauseated. It was difficult even to read with the constant motion.

The tumultuous rocking of the ship found its way into my dreams. My home shook with the movement of the sea; rooms I had walked my whole life suddenly listing, trinkets tumbling from shelves, tapestries flapping in a salty gale, revealing rot and decay on the walls beneath. Or I was atop the Wall, my feet slipping out from under me, snow-white stones rushing to meet me like waves, swallowing me up, filling my lungs with icy rock fragments. I woke screaming more often than not, but the creaking of the ship and the rush of wind and waves drowned out my voice, and Eytan did not come for me. Nor did I tell him of the dreams.

Eventually, my cabin seemed a part of the nightmare, and restlessness and curiosity won out over my tender stomach. Before arriving at the docks, I had never seen the ocean, and now it was all around us. The small window in my cabin did not reveal enough of the waters to sate me. So I made my way gingerly out onto the deck, where I retched over the side almost immediately. I forced myself to stand straight and breathe deeply. And in an instant, I forgot my seasickness. I forgot my body altogether, for I had never seen anything so incredible. Everywhere I looked, there was only ocean.

"Breathtaking, isn't it?"

I turned to Eytan with wide eyes. "I did not know the world had this much water!" I wanted to kiss him right then and there for showing me such a sight. I felt our smiles were mirror images.

His voice became tender. "I wish I could show you everything there is to see in this world."

"Why can't you?" I knew instantly that I had said the wrong thing. His smile faltered; his eyes grew sad.

"Maybe someday."

I cleared my throat and slipped my arm through his. "I am making some progress on those inscriptions," I told him, working to keep my voice casual. "One of the histories of Gaerwn makes reference to them as ancient runes. It seems they were thought to contain some kind of benevolent earth magic. Given time, perhaps I could decipher them."

"Well, we have three more weeks at sea. With your determination, I suspect you'll manage it before we disembark."

The compliment made my heart swell with pride, but I still worried over Eytan. Whatever weighed on him was not something I could ease with my books, or even with my newfound skills at the dagger. I suspected it was something only he could resolve. In all that had happened to me, nothing made me feel so powerless as watching his struggle.

Zav was even less fond of the ship than I. He made piteous noises down in the hold, despite Eytan's frequent visits to him while I had been unwell, and the ship's crew grew anxious and afraid of him. But I was finally getting what Eytan called my sea legs; I felt well enough at ease to walk the deck at length and had not been ill in days. So I brought Zav above deck, hoping the fresh air would help him, but he only lay down on the rough planks, moaning.

"M'lady," a young deckhand said. He held out a finely woven net. "Perhaps this will soothe your beast?"

"You wish to restrain him?" I asked sharply.

"Oh, no! No, m'lady, you misunderstand. I thought we might catch some fish for him. Perhaps the fresh meat will do him good."

"Oh, I see." I flushed. "I'm sorry, I did not mean to snap. Yes, perhaps you are right. But ..."

"Yes?" The young man looked at me hopefully.

"Well, I haven't any idea how to catch fish."

He laughed a deep, rich laugh, his mouth open wide. His smile was contagious. "Why no, of course not. But if m'lady wishes it, I could show you."

The young man taught me how to cast the net while keeping hold of the handlines attached to it. He threw it and hauled it back several times so I could see how it was done, and then passed the net to me.

"What if I drop the line?" I asked.

"Then I'll have to go for a swim!"

We both laughed.

I could not throw the heavy net as far as the deckhand with his strong arms, but I tried my best, and we both watched the net sink below the surface, weighed down by the stones bound to its corners.

"Now, we wait a bit," he said. "It's not the best way to fish in waters this deep, but there's many a fish in these parts. Soon, we'll have ourselves a feast."

I wondered what other ways there were to fish, but I did not want to appear foolish, so I kept the question to myself. In any case, the deckhand was right. Soon, he prompted me to haul the net back in, but it was far too heavy, and it took the two of us together, laughing and grunting, to haul in the fish we had caught. We hoisted our prizes onto the deck, and Zav perked up immediately, nosing around at the gasping fish.

"Go on," I told him, breathless. "We'll do the work. You just enjoy your lunch, your majesty."

Zav glanced up at me, sniffed, and then took a large silver fish whole into his mouth, sending my new friend and me into a gale of laughter. It took me some time to realize that Eytan was watching us, a conflicted look on his face.

Eytan was distracted and withdrawn for much of our voyage, so I befriended the crew. When they had time, they taught me sea shanties, knot tying, useful phrases in half a dozen languages, and many other things. When they were busy with their tasks, however, I practiced with my daggers and spent hours poring over the books Eytan had prepared for me. The symbols I had copied down in Oro were becoming familiar to me. I could sound out the entire alphabet by the end of our second week at sea, and by the third week, I was making progress with my translations, using sample sentences from the history books as my key.

When I finally came to understand the meaning of the sentences in my journal, I shouted so loudly in my excitement that it brought Eytan running to my cabin.

"Julia! Are you all right?"

"Yes, come in, come in!"

"What's happened?" he asked, the worry on his face giving way to confusion.

I held up the book that had been balanced on my knees. Several others lay strewn about my writing desk, weighted open on the pages I required with inkwells and unlit candles and anything else I could find to hold them fast. My fingers were stained with ink, as was the journal in which I was feverishly writing my translations.

"The writing," I told him breathlessly. "I know what it says."

"You deciphered a lost tongue ... in three weeks? You are joking."

I dropped my gaze. "You're the one who told me I could manage it," I murmured, hurt.

"Oh, no, I didn't mean ..." Eytan dropped to one knee beside me. "I did not mean to doubt you. I'm simply surprised. And impressed. I told you that to cheer you up. I did not think *anyone* could manage it."

I flashed a smile to show I forgave him for misspeaking. "Well, *I* did."

He leaned his elbow on the arm of my chair. "So, what does it say?"

Clearing my throat for dramatic effect, I read out:

In these twilight halls there walk
Two young warriors fair
Light of skin and dark of eye
Ebony their hair.

Dead upon the battlefield
Younger than their years
Preserved these two young warriors were
By their people's tears.

Should you come upon them
When your travels take you hence
Remember them as allies
And a gift they shall dispense.

And if you ever are in need
Two words will see you safe
Close your eyes and wish for them
And speak their hallowed names.

We were both silent for a time, as if the words had cast some spell upon us. And perhaps they had, for the reverence I felt simply in reading them aloud was like nothing I had felt before.

"Two warriors," Eytan said finally.

"With ebony hair," I added.

"Twilight halls ..."

"Two young warriors, with dark hair, walking twilight halls," I was speaking swiftly in my excitement, "who dispense gifts! Eytan, it speaks of Malek and Maeve. They are ... they are—"

"Spirits," Eytan finished for me. "I thought it odd that I could not remember Oro clearly, from my visit with my father. I thought it was their parents who had hosted us, but it was them. It was always them ... And the things they knew. The things they could do ... It was more than magic."

"Incredible," I whispered.

"Yes," Eytan said. "You are." This time it was he who kissed *my* cheek. "I've never known anyone capable of what you've just accomplished. You truly are special, Julia."

Special. It was a word I never would have thought of to describe myself.

That night, I awoke in the darkness, shivering. Someone was calling my name. My *true* name. Fear gripped me. How could anyone here know that name? But the voice that called me was gentle and sweet ... and familiar.

"Mother?"

I slipped from my bed. It was her. I knew her voice. Across the room, in the folds of my cloak, something was glowing. A milky, pearly light spilled out through the layers of thick fabric, impossibly bright. It was the vial my mother had given me the day I left the Wall, the day I left her. I had nearly forgotten it. The light had not shone since the night I felt her pass. Could I have been mistaken? Perhaps she had only been ill, and now, with her strength returned, the light too had renewed itself.

She called my name again.

I slipped the chain over my neck and let the vial settle on my chest, impossibly light given its size. I left my cabin and followed my mother's voice above deck. The wind whipped at me as soon as I emerged. It tore strands of hair loose from my plait to whip at my eyes and snaked under my night-shift, its icy touch upon my legs. The deck was damp beneath my bare feet, and sea spray bit at my cheeks and stung my eyes. But still, my mother called.

"Mother!" I shouted against the sounds of ship and sea. "Where are you?" I held the vial out before me to light my way. Out of the corner of my eye, something flickered. A wing, satin black against the velvet black of night. I spun to track it, but I could see nothing. Then, behind me, impossibly close, the sound of feathers rustling, of great wings flapping at the air. I turned again. There was still nothing but the wind.

"Mother!" I screamed.

She was moaning now, weeping, still calling my name. And somehow I knew that she was in the water.

I lurched to the side of the ship and peered over into the inky waves. Thrusting the vial out before me, I searched the sea for any sign of my mother. She was there, I knew she was there. I leaned further. The vial was suddenly a leaden weight around my neck, pulling me forward towards the sea, but I did not care. She was in those freezing waters somewhere, calling for me. She was drowning.

Another voice reached me, from somewhere far off, a bellowing much harsher than my mother's sweet, sad tones. It was calling for someone, but not for me. No, only my mother knew to call for me. Only my mother needed me. But the other voice continued, and it began to sound familiar, and then there was a third voice, horrible and shrill: the raven.

The voices were at war within me, clawing at my head from the inside. The pain was like nothing I had ever known. I let go of the ship to clutch at my skull, and felt myself begin to fall—

There was a blur of motion, and then I crumpled onto the deck, soaking and trembling and nearly blinded with pain. Strong arms encircled me. I forced my vision into focus. It was Eytan, so close I could smell the scent of ink and smoke on his skin. We were on the deck together, his legs tangled up in mine. I could not understand what had happened. The raven's awful voice was gone, but so was my mother's. I began to weep.

Eytan carried me back to my cabin. I was drenched and shivering violently, and I dimly heard him ask for permission to undress me. I suppose I nodded, for he pulled my thin night-shift up over my head, leaving me completely exposed. I did not care. I let him wrap me in thick blankets, let his hand go to my chest, where it moved to take the vial that still rested there. But as soon as he touched it, he winced and jerked his hand away.

"Julia," he said in horror.

I furrowed my brow, looked down, and a new pain overwhelmed me. The vial now glowed a deep, angry red, and beneath it, my skin was seared and blistering. I cried out, but Eytan was already wrapping the vial in a length of cloth and pulling the chain over my head. I could hear myself making pained, disjointed noises. I struggled to take in breath. And then I fainted.

When I awoke, my chest was wrapped in bandages and my body in blankets. Eytan was asleep beside me, sitting upright on the floor of my cabin, his arm and head resting on my mattress. My mouth felt full of cobwebs, and I was too bleary to try to speak. Gingerly, I lifted a hand that did not want to obey. I ran my fingers through Eytan's hair to rouse him.

He awoke immediately and sprung to sit on the bed by my side. "Julia!" He pulled the blanket back over my exposed arm and felt my forehead. His voice broke when he tried to speak. "I was so afraid for you."

I tried to smile, but it became a grimace of pain. "Water," I rasped.

He helped me to sit and lifted a cup to my lips. I was vaguely aware that beneath the blankets, I was still naked, save the bandaging. Eytan must have tended to me himself. I blushed thinking about what he must have seen.

"You don't seem feverish," he was saying. "The burn on your chest is severe, but I used a balm that will soothe it. You will have a scar, though. I'm sorry."

I shook my head. "What happened?"

"You don't remember?"

Tears began to fall before I could even speak. "I was ... dreaming," I whispered.

"You were sleepwalking. It's lucky I was awake. Truthfully I ... I went to your cabin to check on you. When I saw you were gone, I searched everywhere. By the time I came on deck"—he paused, his expression pained—"you were leaning out over the side. You let go of the rail. You almost pitched straight into the sea."

"Something was calling me," I said numbly.

He shook his head. "I heard nothing."

"No, there was ... I heard my mother's voice. She was calling me. And the raven was there, that foul thing. You must have heard—"

"Julia," he said, and the pained delicacy with which he spoke frightened me as much as anything else had, "there was nothing there."

* * ✳ * *

CHAPTER SEVENTEEN

* ✳ * *

I had long known of the continent of Midbar. After the Lion Boy came to the Wall, I began to research the continent. I read of the sun and sands, of the strange creatures and the rich foods. Long after I forgot the Lion Boy's face, I remembered what I had learned of his homeland. I remembered that that was the land of Zav's birth. I read everything I could of that land. I pored over tomes about the lion populations that roamed from the southern plains, through the arid deserts, and all the way to the great city of Bahir. But never in all that time had I dared to dream I would ever set foot there.

After my near disaster aboard the ship, Eytan had stayed by my side at night, sleeping on the floor beside my bed. Each night before sleep, I asked him to tell me tales of Midbar. I felt like a child again. My excitement grew as my strength returned.

Still, I clung to Eytan as we disembarked. Where the shifting deck of the ship had proved a challenge before, now the solid ground beneath my feet seemed just as difficult to stand upon. Apparently, Zav felt much the same. It took four cowering deckhands to coax him from the ship and onto the docks.

"It will pass," Eytan told me, just as he had when the seasickness had struck me. This time I believed him.

Past the docks was a city made of tents. Each tarp was more beautiful than the last, dyed in vibrant colors and embroidered with delicate patterns. Beneath the tents were merchants selling wares unlike any I had ever seen. Bronze structures with interlacing pieces laid out on one table moved of their own accord, thick carpets hanging within a tent looked more elegant than any tapestry as they rippled in the wind. There were barrels and baskets piled high with mounds of spices in hues I scarcely knew existed. Their smells wafted toward me on a warm, dry breeze.

The people around us resembled Eytan far more than myself. Many had the same tanned skin, the thick, wavy black hair, the rich, brown eyes. Others made Eytan seem pale by comparison.

Beyond the market was only sand.

I had left one ocean behind only to be met with another—from blue waves to bronze. My eyes could not fathom the expanse of it. Eytan slid his hand into mine. He was smiling, and I was glad to see it. His face had been creased with worry since that night aboard the ship.

"We still have a ways to travel. But first, there are a few things I must buy you."

"But I don't need—" I began, but he had already set off into the market. I rolled my eyes, but Zav and I followed.

Eytan brought me to a massive tent filled to the brim with garments. He chose a white tunic and trousers, and handed them to me, pointing to a dressing screen. "You can dress there."

"But I *am* dressed. And you've already bought me more than enough clothing."

"Put them on under your dress," he urged. "Trust me."

I rolled my eyes again but did as he said. The fabric was thin and airy and felt cool against my skin. The trousers were concealed completely by my skirts, but the tunic covered my arms to the wrist and sat high on my neck, covering the exposed skin of my forearms and collar—and the bandage that still wound around my chest, peeking out above my dress. I did not understand. I had already seen many women here, some dressed in fewer layers than I. A few had even boasted bare shoulders or midriffs. What had I to hide?

When I emerged, Eytan held out a scarf to me, a confection of sheer silk, which he wrapped around my neck and over my head so that it shielded my brow and covered my mouth and nose completely.

"What is this?" I asked, my voice ringing clear through the thin fabric. "Are you trying to hide me?"

Eytan laughed so loudly that several people in our vicinity turned to look. I could feel my cheeks grow red, but it made no matter. The scarf hid the crimson.

"Julia, look at your hands." I frowned but did as he said. "Now look at mine."

I raised an eyebrow at him, trying to make my impatience known despite how much of my face was hidden.

"Do you see how dark my hands are? Even I must wear protection against the desert sun. Now look at your hands. You have skin like moonlight. What do you think would happen to your skin if the sun were to beat down on it long enough?"

I recalled a pale, freckled kitchen boy who had fallen asleep in the sun one summer back at the Wall. He had returned inside with his skin peeling and blistering, so violently red it made him feverish. But I had never felt anything of the kind.

"Oh," was all I said.

"May I pay for your garments now?" Eytan asked.

I nodded silently. My cheeks were still hot with embarrassment, and I was suddenly very glad for the scarf.

Past the tent city, an escort awaited us. There was a horse-drawn litter and several mules laden with supplies, but there was another animal I could not name. It was the color of the sand, with long legs and an arched back that looked like a sand dune in miniature. A man sat astride it, and he bowed to Eytan, who nodded back to him. Attached to the back of the litter was a simple wooden cart with a white tarp stretched over it. Inside the cart, I could see a trough of water and a massive platter piled high with raw meats.

"For Zav?"

Eytan nodded.

"You prepared all this?" I asked as I nudged Zav into the cart. He went willingly, drawn by the smell of the meat, but paused to nuzzle my face. I patted his nose, and he turned to his feast.

Eytan shrugged. "I sent a missive ahead with Kes. I wanted to make the journey easy for you."

The man on the tall creature cleared his throat, bowing to Eytan again. He inclined his head toward the litter. Eytan took my hand, and we climbed inside. The litter was plush, filled with cushions embroidered in rich colors and shimmering threads. Silk curtains were drawn to keep out the sand, but through their sheer fabric, I could see the rolling dunes and the impossibly blue sky. It was stuffy, though, and only grew hotter as the combined heat of our bodies filled the small space. We were not moving quickly enough to create a breeze.

"How long will we travel like this?" I asked after a few hours.

Eytan cringed. "You won't like the answer."

Crossing my arms over my chest, I gave him a playful scowl.

"Oh, very well," he said. "It is two weeks to Bahir. We—"

"Two *weeks*? We must sit in here for two *weeks*?"

"You see?" Eytan crossed his arms, mirroring my posture. "I knew you would react like this. I sent for a grand litter for us, just to keep you comfortable. Yet still, you complain." He cocked his head, examining me as if I were something in need of appraisal. "You are quite spoiled, you know."

He said it in jest, at least mostly, but it still stung. I had never asked to be locked away my entire life, knowing only my small, comfortable world. Eytan saw the hurt on my face and started to apologize, but I did not want either of us to be so serious. We needed a bit of levity after everything that had happened. So I kicked him in the shin and stuck out my tongue.

Eytan yelped, sounding very much like a small child, or perhaps a pup, and I could not contain my laughter. He laughed too.

The days in the desert were hotter than I had known the world could be, and we stopped often to rest and drink. The nights, however, were bitterly cold. I shivered even under furs, curled up beside Zav and sheltered by the tent our escort pitched each night. There seemed to be no reprieve from the heat but the frigid night, and no reprieve from that icy sleep but the sweltering days. I longed for a breeze. My layers of clothing were soaked through with sweat that dried and froze each night, only to be compounded upon the next day.

I tried not to complain. I did not want to seem spoiled.

What I wanted, suddenly, more than anything, was to ride the horse that led our party. I imagined the wind in my hair as we galloped through the sands, how refreshing it would be. But, though I had ridden Zav countless times, a horse was a different beast altogether, and I had no idea how to ride one.

"Do you know how to ride?" I asked Eytan on our third—or maybe fourth—day of travel. I'd already lost count. I felt constantly dizzy and thirsty, but still, I was determined not to complain.

He looked at me, bemused. "Ride what?"

"A horse, obviously!"

"Yes, of course I do." He paused. "Don't you?"

I shook my head. "I thought maybe ... maybe while we were out here, you could teach me."

It took Eytan quite some time to overcome his astonishment at my riding ignorance. He had just asked me for the hundredth time how I had lived eighteen years without ever learning to ride a horse, and I had just vowed never to speak to him again, when there came a shout from outside our litter. Eytan's men were calling to each other in their own tongue, and while I could not understand their words, the meaning was clear: something was terribly wrong.

Suddenly, everything seemed to happen at once. Swordplay sounded outside the litter. Zav let out a roar unlike any I had ever heard from him before. The litter lurched and I fell to the floor, landing hard on my wrist. I heard a whistling I could not place and, not a moment later, a horrible, meaty sound—damp and deep and somehow reminiscent of hot pain. Somewhere, a man cried out, but I barely heard him. My hearing was flooded with the gurgling gasp that came from just outside our litter. We stopped moving, and I knew that our driver was dead.

Eytan strung his bow and notched an arrow, twitching the curtain aside a fraction to peer out into the sand and screams. "Your blades," he hissed, even as he loosed the arrow and notched another.

I drew the weapons and held them at the ready, though my left wrist smarted, but there was no enemy for me to fight. Our caravan had been comprised entirely of strong men and women who might have been soldiers. It seemed that they had taken on whatever opponents were attacking us. The fighting was all around us, but I could see only shapes through the shroud of silks. The soldiers of our caravan were keeping the attackers at bay, but I did not know for how long. Were Eytan and I simply waiting for our own execution?

"We have to help," I whispered, and my voice sounded desperate in my ears.

"Not yet. We wait until they let their guard down and approach the litter. Then we strike."

"You mean after they've killed everyone else?"

Eytan gave me a look I could not read—part fear, part determination, part ... rage. It frightened me far more than the attackers outside.

* * ✳ * *

CHAPTER EIGHTEEN

* * ✳ * *

Eytan continued to fire arrows from inside the litter. I was sure that whoever was outside must have realized by now where the bolts were coming from, but perhaps it was all too hectic to tell. It sounded more than hectic. It sounded like hopelessness and fear and pain. I wanted to weep.

I could tell when the last of our escort fell. There was a horrible silence upon the hot, dry air that seemed to last for years. And then it was broken by a vicious growl from Zav, a roar, a shout, a scuffling, and then a yelp. Eytan clapped his hand over my mouth before I could cry out.

My Zav ... had they just killed my Zav?

I wept then, clutching my chest. I thought I would retch, from the fear and from the stench of blood. My body was trembling. I could not still it. Eytan removed his hand from my mouth and pressed my dagger back into the hand that still clutched at my breast.

I shook my head to say, "I can't."

His eyes bored into mine. They said, "You can."

He had drawn his blade.

But through the sheer curtains of the litter, there was no movement to be seen. There were no silhouettes approaching us. There was nothing but still-ness, and a silence that threatened to suffocate us both.

"Stay here," Eytan said, so softly it was little more than an exhalation of breath. With his sword held aloft, he pushed aside the curtains and stepped out onto the sand.

In that moment, I felt I had lost him, and I knew suddenly that if he died, I would die too. I had no name for that connection.

Abruptly, I heard the horrible sound of wings, but it died away almost as soon as it had begun.

"Julia," Eytan said, his voice soft, cautious, but ringing out through the silence. "Come out."

There was no enemy. In fact, there was nothing. No bodies, no blood, no horses or tall hump-backed creatures. Our supplies were gone. The caravan and everyone in it had simply vanished. Only the litter remained. The litter, and—

My heart soared. "Zav!"

He limped towards me, holding his left front paw gingerly aloft. I threw my arms around him, and I could do nothing but sob.

Eytan scouted the area, walking a wide perimeter on foot but never straying out of sight. I searched around the litter for signs of a struggle, but impossibly, there were none. We had heard the battle. I had heard men and women die. Yet there were no dead bodies. There was no blood upon the litter or in the sand. There was no evidence at all that anyone but Eytan, Zav, and I had ever stood where we now stood.

I could not understand it. "It must be some sort of dark magic," I called to Eytan as he trudged back toward me through the sand.

"I've never seen anything like this," he replied.

"But you *did* see them, didn't you? When you fired arrows at them from inside the litter?"

His expression looked pained. It seemed he could not explain himself any better than he could explain our circumstances. "I ... I thought I saw ..." he shook his head. "It's as if the memories are fading even as I talk about them."

"But we had a caravan. Soldiers and supplies and horses and ... and hump-backed ... things."

"Camels," he supplied, a smile tugging at the grim line of his lips.

"Yes, and camels! How could all of that have disappeared? And how could we hear a battle but see no signs of it? And why is everything else gone, but somehow Zav is still here?" I twined my fingers tightly in his mane as I asked this last question, frightened that voicing it would somehow make him disappear as well. But he stayed solid beneath my touch.

Eytan patted Zav between the shoulder blades, and Zav gave a great, happy purr.

"You know, I think Zav might have a little magic of his own." He knelt to inspect Zav's paw. Tearing off a piece of his tunic, he wound it around the injury. "Just a sprain, I think," he murmured as he worked. Zav did not complain. "As for the other questions, I've all the same ones running through my mind. As you said, it must be some kind of dark magic. The real question is, to what purpose?"

"Whatever it was, it kept us alive for a reason."

"I agree." Running his hand through his hair, he added, "I wish we had Kes. We could send a missive, ask for reinforcements."

"Where *is* Kes?"

"He should have found us by now. It's possible that whatever force attacked us is somehow keeping him away."

I looked out across the dunes, shielding my eyes against the harsh sun. "You can navigate this desert, can't you?"

He nodded.

"Well then, there is only one thing we can do."

Eytan raised an eyebrow at me.

I licked my lips, the dusty feeling in the back of my throat reminding me of how dire our situation was. We could not last long without water, and we had only the small skins on our belts. The rest had been in the supply wagon. But we also could not stay here. I held out my hand to Eytan.

"Walk."

* * *

By nightfall, I could not speak. My mouth was too dry, my body too light. My head was spinning. I was sure Eytan felt the same. His dark skin had taken on a sickly pallor, and his lips were a thin, cracked line. Zav moaned a low moan.

I did not know much about deserts, but I thought that there must be water somewhere. We had seen a few birds overhead, and here and there a lizard or a snake. If there was life here, I reasoned, there must be water. *There must be water.* I said it to myself over and over as we stumbled along. *There must be water.*

Eytan had chosen our path, determining direction by the movement of the sun, and now he was mapping our movements by the stars. I wanted to ask him to teach me, but I did not have the energy.

I did not remember sinking to my knees. One moment, I was walking, the next, Eytan was kneeling beside me, one hand on my cheek. Was he trembling, or was I? Perhaps we both were.

He did not speak. He simply drew me back to my feet and snaked an arm around my waist, supporting me, but also supporting himself. The sun was rising. I wondered if we would die here.

The sun had already reached its peak in the sky and was beginning to travel downward once more when I saw the small creature. I thought I was hallucinating. It was pale as the sand, almost white in places, with large, pointed ears. At first, I thought it was a cat, but then perhaps it was a fox. Whatever it was, it certainly needed water to survive, and I meant to follow it. I grabbed Eytan's wrist and pointed. His eyes widened. He nodded. He put a finger to his lips and motioned for me to stay still. He crept forward. The cat-fox disappeared over a ridge and Eytan disappeared after it.

I waited.

Days could have passed before Eytan returned to me, but when I saw him appear again at the top of the dune, I knew it could not have been that long. If it had been, I would be dead already. I thought this, and then my eyes refocused, and my only thought was of the wide smile on Eytan's face. His cheeks were glowing, his lips looked full again, and the sleeves of his tunic ... the sleeves of his tunic were damp!

He held a swollen skin of water in his hand.

I would have wept had there been moisture enough in my body for tears. Instead, I scrambled forward on all fours. Eytan skidded down the slope of the dune to meet me, and cradled my head in his arms, pouring water into my mouth as if I were an infant unable to drink by myself. And perhaps I was unable, for as the water passed my lips, I collapsed into his arms, drinking deeply until he pulled the skin away.

"More," I rasped, but he shook his head.

"Wait. Take it slow."

I drank until I felt my head begin to clear, and then I returned to Zav, who was lying in sand the color of his fur, watching us with his chin on his paws, waiting. I let water drip from the skin onto his nose, and he lifted his head, his ears perking up. He made a desperate sort of rumbling sound.

"Here," I whispered. "You'll be all right now." I began to trickle water from the skin, and he opened his great jaws to allow me to pour the water directly into his mouth. Between the two of us, we finished the entire skin, and then Eytan led us to the oasis.

"I'd almost given up hope."

He nodded. "So had I."

We were eating dates that grew on a tree beside the small pool of water. Nearby, the cat-fox watched us, wary, but unwilling to leave her source of life. Zav ignored her, which surprised me. I knew he must have been ravenous.

"What is she?" I asked, motioning to the creature.

"A desert fox," Eytan replied. "You have incredible eyes, Julia. Most people wouldn't have spotted her. If you hadn't, we could have died of thirst by now."

I smiled. I knew we weren't out of trouble yet, but we had food and water for the first time in over a day. All I felt now was relief.

We drank as much as our bellies would hold, filled our skins to the brim, and picked the small tree clean of dates. Eytan picked the blooms off it as well, and a few of the smaller leaves. He explained that the leaves were edible when young, but they looked tough and unappetizing to me. Still, if they would keep us alive until we could find civilization, I would not complain.

We set off once more in the direction of Bahir. We would never make it all the way on foot through this desert; we had still been more than a week away by caravan when we were attacked. But Eytan said that there were settlements and small camps of nomads in the deserts surrounding the great city. We could find aid there and send another missive to Bahir. I just hoped we found such a settlement soon.

Two more days passed. Eytan rationed our food and water, but I knew we would soon run dry again. We shot down birds for Zav to eat, but we had no fire to cook them for ourselves. Even if we had, Eytan would not have partaken. We barely spoke. We walked at night when it was cooler, and slept during the day when the sun was so hot it seemed to bake the sand around us. I wondered if this was what it would feel like to be a loaf of bread in an oven. Even under my layers of clothing, I could feel my skin burning.

On our fourth night without the caravan, I saw something in the distance. The moon was high, and its light turned the golden sands of day to silver and onyx. Rising up out of the earth were jagged structures, like crooked teeth on the horizon. I pointed, and the wide grin Eytan gave me in return brought hope back to my heart.

"Bless your eyes."

The settlement seemed abandoned. Buildings made of stone and packed earth stood empty and crumbling. As we entered the village, it was as if we had crossed an invisible barrier. Suddenly my legs felt heavier. My stomach turned. A sour, acrid taste filled my mouth. I glanced to Eytan, but he did not seem to feel it.

"There should be a well in the village square. Let's pray it hasn't dried up." He laced his fingers through mine, and where our skin touched, my body calmed. But while my hand now felt secure, the rest of my flesh continued to squirm. I felt like thousands of insects were crawling just beneath my skin.

I tried to shake off the feeling. It was probably a combination of the heat, the thirst, the hunger, and the searing of the sun.

We found the settlement's well, shaded by a hut made of palm fronds like the ones of the date tree at the oasis. I longed to be back there. This place brought me no joy, even with the prospect of water. Something in this village was ... *wrong*.

Eytan did not feel it, I could tell. He rushed to the well and lowered the bucket into it, sighing with relief as the sound of a splash echoed back up to us.

"We shouldn't drink it," someone said. It took me a moment to realize it was my own voice.

"What? Julia, our supply is all but gone." He began to haul the bucket up. "This is fine to drink."

"We shouldn't drink it," I said again. "We shouldn't be here." I began to walk without consciously deciding to move. Something was drawing me toward a structure at the far side of the village. It swam in my vision—a long, low building with an arched roof of dried palms. Out of the corner of my eye, I saw something flicker, like a black flame, like wings.

Something hissed my name.

I entered the structure, walking into inky blackness. I heard the manic beating of wings and claws scrabbling on the roof above.

"Julia," someone—something—rasped, drawing out each syllable. "Liar ..."

"Who are you?" My voice rang out clear, stronger than I felt. My gaze was fixed ahead, I felt I could not look back. Zav and Eytan were not at my side. Perhaps they had followed me, but now I could not feel their presence. I knew I was alone.

I gathered my courage. "Show yourself," I said, but I was not sure I wanted to see.

A figure began to emerge from the murky shadows, resolving itself from the darkness as if it had lit a pale flame in its center. But there was no flame, no candle, just a sickly white light emanating from the creature before me. A woman.

Her head was bowed, but what I could see of her features looked like those of a young woman. Yet her pale skin was like ash and parchment: dry, brittle, flaking away in places, revealing a nothingness beneath. She reminded me of a birch tree in winter. Her black hair hung in stringy locks around her face. She wore a white tunic that left her white legs bare. Her feet were bare as well, and their soles were cracked, bleeding, but the blood was inky black.

She was chained to the wall.

"You are a thief," she said.

Her skin was broken where the chains had bitten into her wrists. The same inky blood trickled down her forearms as she shifted her weight, her feet digging into the packed earth beneath us both.

The sound that came from her mouth then might have been a laugh, but it sounded dull and ill-used, as if she had forgotten how. I feared her, but I also pitied her.

"Do you need help?"

She looked up then. Her eyes grew wide. They were completely white, but they looked right at me. Her mouth hung partway open, revealing impossibly white teeth, luminous, like the pearls of her eyes. But her tongue was horribly black.

"Help?" She said the word as if she did not know how to fit it in her mouth. "Help from a thief?"

"I have not stolen anything." I glanced over my shoulder, hoping desperately to find Eytan standing just behind me. But there was nothing there. Truly nothing. The walls of the building had fallen away; there were no longer beams or palm leaves above my head, there was no longer earth beneath my feet. The entrance was gone, leaving only impenetrable darkness where it had been. There was no light whatsoever, save what radiated from—

I cried out as I turned back to the woman. She was standing now, straining against her chains, her torso jutting as far forward towards me as her restraints allowed.

"You," she said slowly, "you stole *everything*. You are a liar. You are a lie. You stole your own name."

* * ✳ * *

CHAPTER NINETEEN

* * ✳ * *

She smelled as she looked: of parchment, wood, and ink. She smelled old—no, ancient. But there was something else. She smelled familiar.

"You know me," I said.

She smiled a tight-lipped smile. Before I could stop myself, or even wonder at my actions, my hand flew up, and my fingers brushed those pale lips.

"I know you."

Her brow knitted. She opened her mouth once more, and I felt her soft breath upon my fingertips. It was cold. She relaxed against her restraints, sinking once more to the black nothingness that was the ground.

"Yes," she said, almost to herself. "I know you. You know me. Though we've never met. We will … never meet." She met my gaze again. "You are your mother's daughter. You are your sister's sister. You are … you are your sister."

Her words sent a hollow ache through my chest, but they were only the truth. Yes, there had been guilt curled around my heart like a sleeping spider, now spreading its spindly legs to stand and weave its web. Yes, I had stolen my sister's name. I had left my parents. And in leaving, I had, it was possible, killed my mother.

"Am I cursed?" I whispered. I could feel the tears stinging my eyes, gathering in corners where they would dry into that spider's web and obscure my vision forever.

"Yes." She reached out to me, hesitated, then rested a trembling hand on my cheek. Her skin was cool to the touch but softer than I had expected. "But you were always cursed. Long before your theft." Her eyes grew mournful. "She tried to save you, to spare you. But she failed. She only delayed the inevitable. It will never stop. It will never leave you in peace. It will pursue you, wherever you may flee. And eventually, it will kill you."

"Why?" I choked out.

She shook her head, and a shiver went through her body. Her toes curled, her fingers curled. Slowly, she curled into herself. I knew, somehow, that she was leaving.

I put my hands on her cheeks. "Wait," I said. "Please."

"You look very much like her, you know. I so longed to see her face again. I am sorry."

I was alone, in a low hall with moonlight streaming through the gaps in the palm-leaf roof. The only evidence of what had passed was a single tear drying on my fingertip.

Someone stumbled into me from behind, and I yelped. But it was only Eytan, with Zav close behind him.

He righted himself and said, "Julia! What *was* that?"

"Could you see her too?"

"See who? There was only you. Standing there without moving for … it must have been hours. I couldn't touch you. It was like there was some barrier between us … like I was seeing you through glass."

There was a note of panic in his voice, so I took his hands in mine. "I'm all right. Don't worry."

Eytan shivered, but I knew it was not from the cool night air. "Maybe you're right," he said. "We shouldn't be here."

From nearby, from right behind him, from just out of the limits of our sight, came a great flapping of wings, and a voice that chilled my blood croaked,

"You are right."

And then the earth crumbled away beneath our feet, and we fell.

We landed painfully on hard stone, the clods of earth that had fallen with us doing little to cushion our fall. I darted to my feet, frantically trying to find the bird that had accosted us above. But it was gone.

Was this the pale woman's doing? Somehow, I thought not. I could not explain my certainty, but I knew that she would do nothing to hurt me. At least, not deliberately.

"Eytan?"

"I'm all right," he grunted, rising. Zav was nosing him anxiously. "What happened?"

I turned to meet his gaze. "I met a woman. A woman in chains." My voice sounded hollow in my ears. "Agatha was right. I am cursed."

Eytan took my hand. "If you truly are cursed, we'll find a way to break it."

"We have to find our way out of here first."

We were deep under the earth, I could tell. Though, from the feel of it, we could not have fallen far. Above us was an impossible expanse of blackness, and around us were cavern walls slick with moisture and shimmering faintly, though there was no light source that I could see. The caves led in only one direction. It seemed we had no choice but to follow.

I began to walk, but Eytan stayed me.

"I know this land well," he said softly. "There are no caves here."

"I'm beginning to think that, as long as you are with me, you'll see a great many things that should not be."

"You're right. But I am not leaving you."

I smiled weakly, and we walked into the darkness together: three figures dwarfed by the impossible blackness that engulfed us.

"You said you saw a woman," Eytan whispered. This was a place, we both felt, where it was better not to be noticed. "Was it the same one from your visions? The woman in the snow?"

"No. This ... this was someone new. But very old. She spoke of me and

my mother, and my—" I stopped myself before I could say the word "sister."
Clearing my throat, I continued. "I don't think she was alive. Not properly.
She was trapped somehow. And I think she knew my mother."

Eytan nodded slowly. "Maybe she has answers for you."

We trudged onward in silence for a while.

"But we spoke so briefly," I said finally. "You said it was hours that I stood
there, but to me, it was mere minutes. I wish I knew how to find her again. I
have so much I need to ask her."

"What did she look like?" Eytan asked, furrowing his brow.

I told him. As I spoke, I could see her so clearly in my mind it was almost
as though she was before me once more. I could see her pearl-white eyes and
teeth, her papery skin. I could feel her lips on my fingertips.

When I finished speaking, Eytan remained silent beside me. The cave
around us had narrowed, and Zav had to walk behind us now.

"Well?" I asked.

"I know of this woman." Eytan's voice was hoarse. His words raised the
hairs on my arms, and I shivered. "For many years now, travelers have spoken
of a forest in the desert. They say that they become lost in the dunes, and the
sun and stars disappear. They cannot navigate. Then, suddenly, they are in a
forest of thin, white trees with black gashes upon their bark. They wander for
days or weeks or months, never sleeping, never eating, lost amongst the trees.

"They say that, just when they feel they can survive no longer, they see a
strange woman, with skin like the trees. She speaks to them, and she weeps,
and she lets them drink her tears. Then the trees vanish, and she vanishes with
them. After that, the travelers return home, but they are never the same. Some
say the forest in the desert has driven them mad. Some say the woman has. But
no one knows who she is, or from where she came."

I wanted to weep then. I wondered if the woman had driven me mad as well,
though I had not drunk her tears. I rubbed my forefinger.

"I saw no forest," I told Eytan.

He shrugged. "You are no ordinary traveler."

I was wary of drinking the water Eytan had pulled from the abandoned well, but it seemed we had no choice. We took a small sip each, gave a trickle to Zav, and continued to walk. Eytan produced date leaves for us to chew. They were bitter and dry, but they helped my mouth to produce some saliva, and I desperately needed the moisture.

The caves sloped and bent and twisted, but it felt like the walls were moving around us, and we were standing still, although my calves ached from the effort of so much movement, and blister upon blister formed inside my boots. I had thought we would die in the desert. I was almost certain we would die here. I had just opened my mouth to speak, though it seemed pointless to say anything now, when I heard a shriek that echoed through the caves.

The narrow path we were walking had opened up into a vast cavern, and the sound bounced off the walls so that it was impossible to tell from whence it had come. But then, sand began to rain down on us from high above, and before we could even blink the grains from our eyes, seven figures dropped down from the hole the falling sand had left behind.

They fell impossibly slowly, as if their flowing purple robes were buffering their descent. Those robes covered every inch of their bodies, with hoods draped over their heads, and hard, purple masks beneath. Their eyes, glowing through the eyeholes of their masks, were pure white, no pupils, no irises. The fabric of their robes clung tight, and I could see that there were both men and women among them. They held tall spears of black wood, with vicious black blades. All seven shrieked a wordless battle cry as they sailed downward, landing effortlessly on the hard ground, with barely a sound on impact.

Out of the corner of my eye, I saw wings.

Eytan's blade was drawn. I had my daggers at the ready.

"Julia," he shouted. "Fight!"

In an instant, everything Malek and Maeve had taught me disappeared. Suddenly I was just a girl with ill-used daggers in her hands and fear in her heart. One of the women lunged at me, and I tried to recall a blocking stance, but my mind was a blank, my limbs frozen in fear. There was only instinct.

I threw myself to the ground. Her spear caught the wall behind where I had been only moments before. I knew that to stay still was to perish. I scrambled clear of her reach and lashed out at her spear with my dagger. It caught only air.

"Julia!" Eytan roared. He was holding off three attackers. Zav was pinned by three more, snarling at their spears. My Zav ... my lion ...

"Leave him be!" I screamed, and before I had time to think, time to doubt, I flung one of my blades. It turned, end over end, and sunk deep into the flesh between one attacker's shoulder blades. He shrieked, dropped his spear, and fell to his knees. Before I could celebrate my success or feel the weight of my actions, my adversary was upon me again. She lunged with her spear, but I was enraged. I would not let them hurt my lion or my Eytan. I deflected her spear with my remaining dagger, and while she was off balance from her attack, I grabbed the spear by its shaft, heaving it towards me with all my might. The woman came with it, using the forward momentum to her advantage. She did not see my blade slashing at her fingers.

When the spear came free of her ruined hand, I swung it at her head. She fell in a heap, smears of blood splattering the wall behind her and seeping into the gray sand.

I turned to Zav. He had snapped the spear of the assailant my dagger had felled between his jaws, but the other two attackers still had him pinned. I slashed and stabbed with my acquired spear, unsure of my target, but my actions were not in vain. I had stolen the attackers' attention long enough to free Zav from the threat of their spears, and he sprang at them. I did not watch what followed.

I looked to Eytan. Two of his attackers had fallen, and he fought the last woman with a ferocity I had never seen in him before. I slid one dagger back into my boot and wrenched the other free of the dead man's back. Armed now with blade and spear, I went to Eytan's aid. The woman he fought had leaped into the air and was striking downward at him, her spear gleaming deadly in the moonlight that spilled in from above like blood.

My own spear caught her in the soft flesh beneath her arm, even as Eytan drove his sword into her belly. Her spear clattered to the rocky ground, and her body fell after it with a wet *thump*. I sank to my knees, panting. Behind me, I could hear the whimpers of the woman and the man that Zav had torn into. He left them to die, nuzzling me with his bloodied maw. I stroked him without looking. I did not want to see him like that.

Eytan and I took our time in recovering our strength, checking each other for unnoticed injuries. We were relatively unharmed—a few shallow gashes each, a puncture in Eytan's side that he insisted had missed any organs, a deep cut on my back that I had not even noticed before, but which did not reach the bone. I marveled at my consideration of these injuries as minor. Mere weeks ago, I would have been shocked by them. I would perhaps have even considered them mortal.

We tore strips of unbloodied fabric from the dead's clothing. I insisted on tending to Eytan first, and he acquiesced, stripping his tunic off and allowing me to wind cloth around his midriff until the wound was bound tightly.

"Tell me if it begins to bleed through," I told him, making my voice stern.

He rolled his eyes. "Your turn. I think you'll have to ..." Clearing his throat, he mimed undressing.

"Yes, yes," I said. I unlaced my dress and shrugged out of it and my under-tunic, leaving my back and chest bare. "You know," I added, "it won't kill you. It's only skin. And you've seen it before, remember? Aboard the *Aliyah*."

I glanced back in time to see Eytan blush furiously.

Shielding my breasts with my hands as Eytan bound my wound, I stared at a beetle that was making its way up the cave wall towards the moonlight above. Its exoskeleton shimmered in shifting tones of black and blue and purple. I looked up through the gash in the earth, where the sky was visible. I could see only the moon's light, not the moon itself. It was not high enough in the sky yet, I supposed. I was trying not to look at the rippling scar on my breastbone, from that horrible night when my mother's vial had burned—*my mother's vial!*

"Eytan!" I cried.

He started and laid a hand on my bare back. "Did I hurt you?"

"What? Oh, no. No. The vial. My mother's vial."

"What of it?" he asked as he finished wrapping my wound.

"Follow a moon, a beetle, and a vial. That's what Agatha told me, before she ..." I could see the puzzlement in Eytan's eyes. I shrugged my clothes on hurriedly.

"When she prophesized for you?"

"Yes, and look." I pointed at the beetle, at the moonlight spilling in from the hole far above us. "Do you still carry my mother's vial?"

He pulled a roll of fabric from a pouch on his belt and held it out to me. "Be careful."

I took it and carried the bundle to a patch of moonlight that shone on the cavern floor. I wished to be a beetle then, able to climb out of this cave and into the open night air. Careful not to touch the vial with my bare skin, I unrolled it from the fabric, setting it in the pool of moonlight. It shone dimly, and I waited. Nothing happened.

I sighed, sitting back on my haunches, and looked back over my shoulder at Eytan and Zav. "It was worth trying," I said.

Eytan nodded, getting to his feet. He approached one of the dead bodies that still littered the cavern floor, and grabbed her—it?—under the arms.

"What are you doing?"

"Let's put them over here," he said, motioning with his head to a place in the corner, where the blood pooled thick and two dead attackers lay torn apart. It frightened me to think what Zav was capable of, but he had only been protecting himself, and me.

I went to Eytan and took the legs of the body he held. Together, we hauled all the bodies to the far corner of the cavern, piling them unceremoniously atop one another. Though I knew these people had tried to kill us, I felt guilty disposing of them so.

"Have you seen warriors like this before?" I asked Eytan.

He shook his head.

"Maybe they were magic too. Sent by my curse."

"You mustn't feel responsible."

I tried to smile but couldn't. "It's difficult not to. Everything that has happened in this desert, it was the doing of that raven. I think it is some sort of harbinger. I heard it after the caravan disappeared, and in the village, before I found that woman, and when we fell ... and I saw it when those people attacked. I think the curse brought us to this cave on purpose. I think it sent those people and meant for them to kill us."

As if the curse had heard my words, a sighing sound rushed towards us from the direction of the dead. Eytan and I grabbed our weapons. I could feel the gash on my back reopen in my haste. But the dead did not stir. Instead, they began to shrink, deflating. As we watched, they began to decay at impossible speed, filling the cavern with the stink of rot. Their skin fell away, oozed off, soaked into the ground, was gone. After mere minutes, as we held our breath and our hearts pounded, only bones were left beneath suddenly threadbare fabric. The bones turned to dust, and the attackers' robes fell into a heap, withered and ancient, as if they had lain in this chamber for thousands of years.

"How ...?" Eytan breathed.

"I told you. The curse. It ... it *made* them. It is growing more powerful."

"What do we do now?"

I began to pace. "There must be something. There must be some way." I moved to the center of the cavern and peered out at the sliver of sky visible high above. I still could not see the moon; only its indirect light shone in. Suddenly I longed for it. I longed for a ladder or some rope. We could not climb so high without one, not even if the three of us could somehow stand feet (or paws) on shoulders like the acrobats my father had invited to the Wall for my sixteenth birthday.

But then I remembered. "'Close your eyes and wish for them. And speak their hallowed names.'"

Eytan looked up at me as if I were mad. "What?"

"The runes! The last verse of the translation—'Close your eyes and wish for them. And speak their hallowed names.' Malek and Maeve! They can save us!"

I squeezed my eyes shut, clasped my hands together at my heart, and wished with all my will. "Malek," I whispered. "Maeve."

There was no answer but the silence of the night above.

"Malek," I said, louder this time. "Maeve." I turned a slow circle. "Maeve. Malek. I summon you! We need you. Malek! Maeve! Maeve! Malek!"

"Julia," Eytan said sharply. He sat with his back to the wall, a grim look on his face. He shook his head. "It was only a story. They will not come."

I waited. I waited for minutes or hours. But nothing changed. I glanced from my mother's vial, sitting dejected in the light of a moon I could not see, to the rags that had minutes before been robed warriors, to Zav resting his chin on Eytan's thigh. Yes, we would die here.

I climbed into Eytan's lap, leaning my head on his chest, one hand curled around the slope of his strong shoulder, the other buried in Zav's mane.

"Will you ... will you hold me? Until the end?"

He wrapped his arms around me. "I will."

* * ❋ * *

CHAPTER TWENTY

* * ❋ * *

This was the end. My life had only begun months ago, the moment my feet hit foreign soil outside the Wall. And now it was over. I felt I had lived my entire life an insect caught in amber, something the world had looked upon but never touched. Until I left the Wall. Until I met Eytan.

I realized that I was stronger out in the world than I had ever been within the Wall. I had gained strength by leaving, although it may have cursed me, and I gained strength by traveling and learning all the things that I had learned. I had gained strength from Eytan. He made me stronger. And now, he held me in his arms, his chin resting on the crown of my head, and I knew that I could have spent a lifetime with him if I'd been given the chance. But then, in a way, I supposed I had.

I did not know how long it would take to die.

I did not know how much we would have to suffer before the end was upon us. But I was glad to be with him, in this and in all things. Yes, I understood now. I understood the ache in my heart when I looked at him, and when I thought of life without him. I loved him. And I had to tell him the truth.

What will he think of me?

"Eytan, there is something I have to tell you." I pulled away, just enough to look up into his dark brown eyes. I almost lost my nerve, looking into those beautiful eyes. But, taking a deep breath, I forced myself to continue. "My name is not Julia."

There was a sadness in those eyes I could not fathom.

"I know."

I stood, almost involuntarily. "What?"

"Your name ..." Eytan swallowed the hoarseness in his voice. "Your name is Thea."

"How ... how did you know that?"

"Five years ago, I gave you a gift."

My mouth fell open, and for a moment it was all I could do to keep breathing. I felt sick. I tried to speak, but there were too many thoughts rushing about in my head to decide what to say. Finally, I managed one word: "You."

Eytan nodded, with something in his eyes that looked very much like longing.

I waited for him to speak, but he seemed to be waiting for me to produce the same phenomenon, so, in a burst of confused passion, I cried, "You gave me Zav!" It was not an accusation, exactly. It was an epiphany, and I almost laughed at the absurdity of it. For months I had been traveling with a man I knew nothing about, thinking I was being rebellious and grown-up, and it turned out this man was nothing but a boy with a lion!

"Yes," Eytan said, and his somber tone sobered me instantly.

The sick feeling grew in my stomach, and I was almost afraid. "How could you keep this from me?"

"Thea," he said my name, my true name, as if he craved it. As if he had been longing to form his lips around the word since we first met. Perhaps he had been. I could not deny that it sounded beautiful on his tongue. "Thea, five years ago I came to your home because I was fleeing mine. I wasn't ready to be what I now know I must be. Your father sheltered me until I was strong enough to continue on my own. I owed him a debt. My *house* owed him a debt. So I told him to call on me, should he ever need me. When I came of age, he appointed me the knight of your house."

"In Saberhold ... my family crest ..." I trailed off, my mind moving too quickly for my tongue to keep up.

"Yes. So when you left your Wall, your father had word of it, and he called on me to bring you home. It was my duty. I was—I *am* your sworn protector." He shook his head and sighed. "Finding you was easy. But to stop you from living, to drag you from your first freedom ... I couldn't. So I decided to show you the world instead, before I brought you home to be locked away from it." He looked like he might cry, and my heart ached for him, for both of us.

But I was also ... not angry, exactly. Bewildered, frustrated, embarrassed. "Why did you lie to me for so long? Why did you let *me* lie to *you*?"

"You mean your name?"

I nodded. "Among other things."

"That's the only thing you ever lied to me about. And I understood why. It was wise of you, really. There is much damage that can be done to a person if the wrong people know her name. As to why I lied to you ..." Eytan hung his head.

The simple motion nearly broke my heart. It brought me to my knees, and I found my hand on his chin, lifting his face so I could see those dazzling eyes once more. I felt betrayed, yes. But the fear of this revelation was gone. I believed him. And I remembered Agatha's words to me that horrible night: "You have good reason to trust Eytan, though you may not understand it yet." Even then, she had told me Eytan was hiding things from me. Should I have been so shocked?

"It's all right," I whispered. "You and I, we don't have to be afraid of each other. You can tell me. You can tell me anything." My hand moved of its own accord to touch Eytan's cheek.

He smiled and covered my hand with his own. "I lied to you because I did not want you to think you owed me anything. I gifted Zav as much for myself as for you. It was my way of proving I would be *there* for you, even if I could not be *with* you. And the day I saved your life, I wanted nothing more than to tell you who I was, but I was afraid you wouldn't remember me. I was afraid you would give me some hollow thanks and return home. And ... I couldn't bear that."

There were no words to match those that Eytan had just spoken, and even had there been, I was ill-equipped to use them. Instead, I flung my arms around his neck and rested my head on his shoulder. I felt his arms encircle my waist to hold me tightly, but gently, so gently it was like he was a part of me. A few tears escaped my eyes because I was happier than I had ever been before in my life, and because I was frightened, and because I now had more to lose than I had ever imagined I could. But our confessions had come too late. We would die knowing the truth. Was that enough?

"Jul—Thea!" Eytan cried suddenly, awe and excitement coloring his voice. "Thea, look!"

I pulled away reluctantly. What could be so important now, when we were nearing the end of our lives, when there was nothing left for us save one another? But when I turned, I understood, and my heart soared. The moon hung over the hole in the ground above us, finally visible. As its light poured directly into the cavern for the first time that night, it fell upon my mother's vial, and suddenly, the cave exploded in light.

My breath caught. My heart seemed to stop. Time seemed to stop. It was as if we were inside the crystal vessel. Fragmented blue and silver light glowed around us, reflecting our own visages, but also other things: visions, thoughts, memories, dreams. I saw my parents and Julia. I saw the visions and nightmares that had plagued me since I left the Wall. I saw Eytan, young and hungry, trudging towards a grand white wall, leading a lion behind him. I saw a vast forest of birch trees and a young, ancient woman waiting alone. All of this happened in an instant, and it happened for eternity, and then the light collapsed in on itself.

In its place, there was a rope: silver-white, and black where it wound round itself. Eytan scrambled to his feet and tested it. It held his weight. He turned back to me, beaming.

"Now that," he said, "is magic."

He climbed the rope first, hauling himself hand over hand for what seemed like ages. By the time he reached the surface, the rope was smeared with his blood.

"Zav next," he called. "Tie the rope around him, and I'll haul him up. Then I'll throw it back down and pull you up as well."

I shook my head. "You can't pull Zav up alone. He's too heavy."

"What choice do we have?"

My mother's vial sat dully upon the ground. I touched it gingerly and knew somehow that its power was exhausted. I curled my fingers around it and slipped its cord over my neck.

I called Zav to the center of the cavern and tied the rope around him, winding it around his body like a harness, trying to distribute the weight as best I could. I hoped we would not hurt him when we pulled him up. I hoped we were strong enough to pull him up at all. I hoped the rope would hold. Then, I climbed onto his back. He did not complain. We had done this countless times back within the Wall, pretending to be circus folk doing tricks. I could even stand on my hands upon his broad golden back, waving my feet in the air. This was going to be more difficult, though.

"Thea, it's too dangerous," Eytan called from above. I ignored him.

The rope bit into my hands immediately, searing into my skin like the desert sun. I could not keep my grip. I slid back down to Zav's back before I had even made it a quarter of the way up.

"Let me pull you up!" Eytan said.

I shook my head, taking the silken scarf from around my head and neck. I wrapped it around my hands and then around the birch tree rope. And I climbed.

I do not know how long it took. I slipped a few times, sliding back down the length of the rope again before catching myself with my feet. I found that if I wrapped one foot in a loop of the rope, I could use it to push myself up, taking some of the strain off my arms. Still, my muscles burned, and my skin cracked and bled even through the silk. But finally, the surface was in reach, and Eytan's strong arms were hauling me up and out of the cave that would have been our tomb.

We lay panting on the night sand. I looked around. The rope went on for miles, disappearing over a dune, impossibly long. Impossible in all aspects.

"Hurry," I said. "We don't know how long we have before the magic fades."

Together, Eytan and I heaved at the rope, pulling Zav slowly but surely to the surface. As we toiled, I thought it should not have been achievable. I had the feeling that the rope was somehow *helping*. Not enough to make the task easy, but enough to make it possible. The more aware of that I became, the more I could feel the power coursing through the rope. Zav, of course, complained the entire time. I could not help my laughter.

When Zav was safely on the sands, we laid back again and rested a moment before Eytan said, "We need to keep moving."

I nodded and stood. The wound on my shoulder was aching, probably from the effort of my climb. I held out my hand to Eytan, to pull him to his feet. He took it, but when he began to rise, he let out a gasp of pain, falling to his knees again.

I dropped to mine as well. "What is it?"

He held his side. "My injury ..." When he pulled his hand away, it was covered in blood.

Gasping, I pulled his tunic up to examine his wound. It was bleeding through the cloth I had tied there and through his tunic as well. Pulling the cloth away, I recoiled. I could not help it. The wound was black, dark green veins of poison shooting from it.

* *✳* *

CHAPTER TWENTY-ONE
* *✳* *

Eytan groaned. "It's some sort of poison."

"Or more dark magic." I pressed the cloth against his wound, trying to stem the bleeding. His blood was too dark. Its smell was wrong.

"Show me yours," he gasped. "You could be poisoned too."

I slipped my dress and tunic down over my shoulders and Eytan peeled away the cloth. The moment he did, a sharp burning erupted across my skin, and I cried out. How had I failed to notice this pain before? Now it was all I could feel, all I could think of. It was a pain that was visible, dancing before my eyes in strange shapes and hues so I could see nothing else.

Eytan covered my shoulder again, and I fell forward in the sand, on all fours, panting.

"Oh, Thea," he said.

The sound of my name from his mouth still made my heart flutter. It was the only kind sensation I had now.

He helped me dress again, whispering to me. "I'm so sorry. I'm so, so sorry. I should never have brought you here."

I shook my head. "We just have to keep moving." Pointing at the pre-dawn stars, I continued, "You can navigate. Point us towards the city. We'll find some-one. We'll be saved. There will be healers in the city, won't there? They will make us well again. We just need to get there."

Eytan nodded, but I could see his strength fading. He had used all of it in getting us out of that pit. And his wound was deeper than mine, closer to his organs, I thought. The poison seemed to be affecting him more swiftly than it was me. The sun was rising. Soon, the day would be hot and oppressive. I did not know how much time we had.

"Curse this desert," I muttered. "Bad luck since we arrived." I took Eytan's bow and quiver from his back and his sword from his hip. I slung his arm across my shoulders and helped him onto Zav's back. Then I donned his weapons myself. "Zav will carry you," I told him. "We will make it."

The rope that had saved us from the pit had disappeared into the sand, as though it had never been, but Eytan pointed over the sand dune, in the direction the rope had led. That was where we would go. I knew that even had I been without Eytan, the rope would have led me to the right path. We set off once again.

I had no love for this desert. We walked for hours, stopping now and then to drink from our skins of water. We did not have much left. I fed Eytan the last of our dates. He was feverish and weak. I prayed.

I wondered if we would come upon the woman again, if we would see her forest in the desert. I felt that she was dangerous, but I knew also, though I could not explain how, that she meant us no harm. I puzzled over our time in the desert. Back in Gaerwn, the curse had plagued my dreams and played tricks with my sight, showing me those horrible visions, that mysterious woman. But it was not until we were on the sea that it succeeded in physically harming me, using my mother's vial against me and attempting to drown me. It was not until we were in the desert that it managed true feats of magic.

Was it growing stronger with proximity? Was it connected to the woman I had spoken to? *Was* it the woman? She knew my mother. She was lonely and hurt and somehow afraid. I felt in my heart that, in essence, she was kind. Why would she torment me this way?

I felt the woman was with me even now, and it did not make me afraid.

The sky above was pockmarked with roiling clouds. Maybe it would rain. I was thirsty again. My lips were cracked and my throat felt dry and caked with dust. We walked on.

Eytan's bow and quiver were an even weight on my back that thumped in time with every step I took. Pebbles were wearing through my boots. Blood pooled within them from blisters long since ruptured. Looking up, I saw a form in the distance. I stopped. I squinted. On the dusty earth sat a toddler, watching, like a reflection of a younger me. My own green eyes gazed back at me, but the smile was different. Wider, with thinner lips and fuller cheeks. I knew who this was.

Julia.

I called her name. Stumbling forward, I reached for her. "It is not safe!"

Julia giggled and kicked her little feet in delight. She had not aged. How could it be that she had not aged?

"Darling, please. Mother will be waiting—" No. Mother was gone, and Julia was gone. I stopped again and stared at the ethereal child until she began to fade away. I was Julia now.

"Thea?"

I started, turning at the rasp of Eytan's voice. Yes, I was Thea. Not Julia. Thea.

"What did you see?"

"It was nothing."

Eytan shivered. He was weakening quickly, and Zav struggled under his weight, weak as well from hunger and thirst. But I could smell something on the wind, something out of place, and it was not my instincts but my growling stomach that urged me to follow it. I walked in the direction of the wind and the smell, and finally, I saw our salvation.

In the valley below us was another settlement, but this one was full of life. Those great hump-backed camels grazed on small shrubbery, people in sand-colored robes milled about the streets, and smoke billowed from chimneys, carrying the scent of food more strongly now. And farther off, just in sight on the horizon, were vast, gleaming city walls. Bahir.

"Eytan!" I cried. I looked back at him, eager to share with him the hope that I now felt. He was unconscious. My stomach sank. I touched his forehead, his cheek. His skin was hot to the touch, and sweat soaked through his clothing. His face and lips were pale.

"No ... no. Please, hold on just a little longer. We are so close. Eytan, please, just hold on!"

My heart battered my chest and my eyes flitted in desperation. I swallowed, trying to calm myself.

"Zav," I said. "Follow."

And I took off down the slope of the dune at a run.

I stumbled into the village and fell at the feet of the first person I saw.

"Please!" I cried, pointing out at the sands, where Zav lumbered his way slowly toward us. "Please, my friend is hurt!"

The man said something in a tongue I did not speak. He sounded perplexed, waving his arms.

"Please, I cannot understand. Does anyone here speak my tongue? My friend has been poisoned. He is Eytan of Bahir—"

"Eytan?" the man said sharply.

I nodded, snatching his bow from my back. It bore engravings in Eytan's native tongue. I hoped it would help the man understand.

He took the bow from me as though it were something holy, his eyes growing wide. "Eytan," he said again, reverence in his voice. He called over his shoulder to another man nearby, shouting something urgent in their tongue. Then he knelt and handed the bow back to me. Rising, he placed a hand on my shoulder. He squeezed gently, smiling. I understood that he would help us.

The villagers brought us into a massive tent where a brazier in the center made the room stiflingly hot. Incense burned all around us. The men left, bowing to me, and suddenly Eytan and I were surrounded by wizened old women, who stripped us both of our clothes with surprisingly deft hands.

I thought to feel shy, but Eytan was unconscious, and I had nothing these women had not seen before. I averted my eyes from Eytan's form, though, partially for the sake of modesty, and partially because I could not bear to see the green poison that was snaking its way through his veins, turning his bronze skin pale.

The women gasped when they saw our injuries. They wrapped us both in white linens, leaving bare only the gashes on our skin, conferencing with one another the entire time. I wished I could understand their words.

A small girl rushed in, holding a woven basket nearly the size of her body. The women converged upon it. They removed herbs both fresh and dried, bottles of liquids, jars of ointments. I watched in awe, my head spinning, my vision blurred, as they mixed salves, soaking this in water, burning that over a flame. They never hesitated, never wavered. I wanted to learn what they knew.

One of the women approached me, holding out a wide leaf of some sort, upon which she had smeared a brown paste flecked with green and gold. She motioned to my shoulder, raised her eyebrows in a question, and nodded.

She was asking permission.

I nodded back vigorously.

She smoothed the leaf over the gash on my shoulder blade, and I screamed. Pain overtook my consciousness once more, and the last thing I saw before my eyes shut was Eytan's form, shuddering, as old women surrounded him.

I awoke on my stomach, lying on a straw mat, Zav curled up on my left and Eytan asleep on my right. Forgetting my injury, I shot to my knees and reached for him. Dull pain coursed through my shoulder, but it was no longer overwhelming. My head spun with hunger and thirst. I gasped.

"Down," someone said to me, in an accent I had never heard before.

I looked up to see one of the old women. Her weathered brown skin was marked with dark swirls of ink that encircled her fingers, creeping up her hands to disappear beneath her robes and appear again at her neck. I wondered if they covered her whole body.

"Down," she said again. She held her hands out before her, palms down, miming a patting motion.

I eased myself down to lie on my back. "You speak my tongue?"

"Some. Little. No up. Only down."

"I understand." I looked at Eytan. "Is he all right?"

She nodded. "Will heal. Many poison. Takes time."

I closed my eyes, letting the relief flood over me. "When will he wake?" I asked.

The woman shrugged, kneeling between us and feeling both our foreheads. "Not knowing. Day. Days. Difficult."

"Thank you," I whispered.

She smiled, and the kindness in her eyes reminded me of Annie's mother, Sophie, who had helped me back in Gaerwn just after I'd left the wall. It seemed so long ago now.

I smiled back.

"Hungry?" the woman asked. "Food? I give food." She patted my hand and left the tent, returning with what seemed like a feast to me after so many days of hunger.

"Lion eat," she told me. "Meat. Lion like meat."

"I don't know how to repay you."

"Repay?"

"How can I thank you?" I tried to explain. "What can I give you and your village, to thank you for your help?"

She shook her head, looking puzzled. "No thank," she said gently, patting my hand again. "Why thank? You with Prince. We help Prince. We help you."

My eyes widened, and I looked from Eytan to the old woman and back again. "*Prince?*"

CHAPTER TWENTY-TWO

A grand escort brought us to Bahir. Armed soldiers took Eytan first, carrying his unconscious form as though he were the most precious thing in the world. I could hardly argue with that.

I thought at first that they would leave me behind, but once they had settled Eytan into an ornate litter, the soldiers returned for Zav and me, ushering me into a second litter and Zav into a beautifully carved covered wagon. I had never seen so much splendor. No one spoke to me. They bowed and offered me fresh clothing, food, and drink but did not say a word. They eyed my knives and Eytan's sword and bow, which I still carried, with confusion, and perhaps with fear. I was alone. Despite the opulence that surrounded me, I was afraid.

Eytan still had not woken. I worried over him ceaselessly. I wondered when he would wake, and what would happen to me in the meantime. I did not allow myself to think that he might not survive. The old woman had told me he would. I had to trust that.

I heard the massive wooden gates of the city groan as we were admitted into the capital, but when I twitched the curtains of my litter aside, I could see only throngs of people, some waving banners, some holding out offerings, some simply standing with arms outstretched, like they hoped to grasp even the thought of Eytan's presence. My litter was a speck amidst a great procession, and I knew from the smell and the hoofbeats that I was surrounded by many rows of riders. Whether it was for my protection or my containment, I could not tell.

Beyond the escort, the cries of the people of Bahir echoed. There were cheers all around us, cheers that must have been for Eytan, for a prince returned home. *A prince.* I had thought the revelation that Eytan and the Lion Boy were one and the same had come as a shock. The idea that Eytan was a prince was something else entirely. I had thought maybe he was the son of an important merchant like my father was, or perhaps some lower noble at most. Of course, I had surmised that he was a person of influence and means, given how his father wished him to return home and take up his responsibilities, but by that logic, I was a person of influence as well, and I was certainly no princess. A prince ... I could barely even fathom it.

Finally, we left the streets of the city behind, passing through another set of gates that swung open and then shut behind us with an almost musical metallic *clang*, into what I assumed was the palace grounds. I wished I could see more out of my window. Tales of Bahir from my girlhood and stories Eytan had told me over the past few months painted pictures in my mind that I was sure paled in comparison to what really lay beyond my litter. Already, I was anticipating a time when I would be left alone, when I could explore. I imagined wandering the palace grounds on my own, waiting for Eytan to recover. I imagined the two of us roaming the city together—perhaps he would wear a disguise so he could walk amongst his people. What would it be like, to see his childhood home through his own eyes?

But no. That could not be. I had had ample time to consider, and I knew what I had to do, though I dreaded it. I would wait only for Eytan to recover, and then it would be time.

I did not see where they took Eytan. I was led down corridors streaked with sunlight that seemed richer than any I had ever known, and dappled with shadows from the latticed wooden panels that stood in place of outer walls. The tiles beneath my feet were azure and gold and ruby, forming mazelike patterns that were dizzying to look upon but beautiful as well. Stained-glass lanterns splashed a myriad of colors upon the ceilings. It was the loveliest place I had ever seen. Yet my heart ached.

I was admitted to a chamber full of plush pillows, with a bed cloaked in silks. The door closed behind me, and I thought I heard it lock. I waited until the footsteps on the other side receded and turned the heavy circular handle. Yes, I was locked in. What if they blamed me for Eytan's injury? What if I was to remain prisoner here forever? What if I was to be executed?

No, I told myself firmly. Eytan would recover. He would recover soon. He would never stand for me being locked up like this, comfortable a cell though it may be. He knew I had lived locked away for far too long.

Zav was already within our lush prison, hunched beside a dish laden with meats and another of clear water, awaiting me happily. I threw my arms around him. I allowed myself only a moment to weep, and then I explored my chambers. It did not take me long to find what I sought.

The writing desk was on a covered balcony with columns of rich, dark wood and more cushions on its floor. Silk curtains were drawn, softening the light from the courtyard beyond. They were thin enough to see through, though, and I watched servants and courtiers bustling about below. Some glanced up towards me curiously, and I thought of withdrawing inside, but what had I to be ashamed of? I observed them for some time, wondering at the flurry of their comings and goings. Then, fearing I would lose the light, I wrote a letter.

Many days passed with no news of Eytan, and I began to fear I truly was a prisoner. I was confined to my chambers, with little in the way of company and no explanation. Food was brought to me three times a day, and it was rich and plentiful, but delivered by wordless servants who turned deaf ears on my queries. I was brought fresh clothing, in the local fashion. Bright colors and intricate patterns adorned my shift-like dresses, and underneath, light, airy trousers and tunics kept me modest but cool. Every evening, servant girls arrived with pails of water and bottles of oils to bathe me. At first, they were wary of Zav, but by the third evening, they were crooning over him and stroking him. They spoke freely, but only in the local tongue. I knew there were several languages spoken in Midbar, and all had several dialects. I did not know which I was learning, but the girls would chatter and gossip and point to objects and mime actions, teaching me their words for water, skin, cloth, flowers. I tried to ask after Eytan, but at the mention of his name, the girls would only blush and giggle and sigh dreamily.

So I waited. My chambers held many books, but only a few in my own tongue. I skimmed through them, and then busied myself with trying to make sense of those in the tongues of Midbar. But I had little success. I watched the courtyard. I brushed the knots from Zav's mane. I practiced my form with my daggers. I paced. I dreamed.

They were not all nightmares, not anymore. Some of the dreams were of Eytan, others of Julia—the real Julia. But most were of the woman and her forest in the desert. In the night, I closed my eyes and watched her weep. It seemed to me as though she had lost as much as I had. Perhaps even more. She walked among her pale trees, stopping every so often to caress their bark. Where her tears fell, the sand absorbed them, lapping them up, and I could see silver-white veins of light inching into the trees.

In one dream, I found her naked and trembling, kneeling amidst a ruin of snapped branches that seemed to bleed black ink. Her back was to me, and it bore deep gashes that seeped blood as black as the tree sap. Flakes of snow or ash or both floated down upon her, settling in her jet-black hair. I could feel her pain as if it were my own—not just the pain of the lashings, but that of rejection, of loss, of hopelessness and heartbreak so intense they threatened to drown us both. She reached out hands scraped and scratched and gathered the dead branches to her. Under her touch, they turned to rags, and the rags formed into something like a cloak, and she wrapped the cloak around her shoulders, concealing her ruined back. She forced herself to stand with the effort of one who was infinitely weary, and she began to walk. Her bare feet left smudges of black blood in her wake.

After eight days alone in my chambers, a man appeared at the door. It was not time for my meal.

"Come," he said to me, and I did, without hesitation. His somber face terrified me, and in my mind flashed images of Eytan dying, Eytan dead, Eytan gone from me forever.

But the man led me to a chamber that looked to be a council room, hung with maps and charts, dominated by a great wooden table strewn with parchments. And at the head of that table—

"Eytan!" I cried, and I ran to him, flinging my arms around him without a thought to the armed guards who flanked him. He caught me in his arms, chuckling, but he sounded winded. I pulled away to kneel beside him, my hand hovering at his midriff where the poison had begun its campaign. "Are you all right? Are you healed?"

He took my hand and pressed it to his chest. My heart fluttered.

"It's just a little pain," he said. "I'll make a full recovery. If I rest."

"Which he will not," the guard at his right said balefully.

Eytan clapped the large woman on the shoulder. "Orly, I did miss you and your badgering."

"My prince, what is this 'badgering' and how may it aid you?"

Eytan laughed aloud.

The sound made me breathe a sigh of relief. I wanted to stay by his side, to watch him and make sure he was as well as he claimed. I wanted to hold his hand and never let go. But I knew that could not be. Now that I knew Eytan was safe, the time had come for me to go. And where I went next, he could not follow.

"Thea?"

A pang of loss that reminded me of the woman in the desert shot through my chest. Eytan could see my pain, I knew. He could tell something was amiss. I smiled, but tears were forming in my eyes.

"Could we ... could we be alone?"

Eytan led me through the palace corridors and out a nondescript side door that seemed too lowly for a prince to use. He held my hand as we walked, and I could feel his fear that I was slipping through his fingers. It was not misplaced. His guards followed at a distance, but when we reached our destination, he dismissed them, much to Orly's chagrin. She eyed me as if I might reveal myself to be an assassin at any moment, but eventually she left us.

We were in a walled garden replete with desert blossoms and shaded by trees with leaves as large as my entire body. It was unlike any garden I had ever seen, with plants and blooms I had no name for, and it was beautiful. In the center of the garden was a fountain with petals floating on the water's surface. There we sat, on the smooth stone edge, our reflections playing in the cool water until it was difficult to tell where I ended and he began. I wanted to melt into his embrace.

"I'm sorry," he said. "Again."

"You are a prince."

"Yes."

"That is ... quite a revelation."

He chuckled. "I wanted to tell you."

"No, you didn't."

He met my gaze, almost startled. "No," he agreed, "I didn't."

Smiling sadly, I said, "Because you did not want to be a prince at all." I skimmed my fingers along the surface of the water, setting the flower petals on their own disparate journeys. "All the adventuring, the secrecy, the reluctance to come back here ... It was all to do with this. Agatha told me as much, though I did not understand at the time."

He only nodded. We were silent for a long while before he finally asked, "Are you angry with me?"

"No." I surprised myself with how readily I said it. I should have been angry with him, I thought, for keeping so many secrets. But he had never lied to me, not outright, and, as I had told him when we had revealed ourselves to one another in that cavern in the desert, I had kept my secrets too. I cleared my throat, trying desperately to fight back tears. "But ..."

"But?"

I looked up, and the longing in his eyes nearly broke my resolve. I told myself I must be strong and tried to believe I could be. I reached into the pocket of my dress and produced the letter I had written, folded and tear-stained, from within. I slipped it into his hand.

"I am leaving," I said, feeling like I was choking on the words. My voice was so faint I thought, at first, he had not even heard me.

"You are ... leaving? But why?"

I smiled through the tears that had refused to stay behind my eyelids. "It's all there," I said. "In the letter." He made to unfold it, but I stayed his hand. "No. Not until ... not until I've gone. Please."

There were tears in his eyes as well. "I don't understand."

The tears were coming faster now, tickling my cheeks and staining my lips with salt. "I must go at once. If you could, please have someone escort me and Zav from the city, and provide us with provisions for the desert."

His eyes widened. "You're going *alone*? Jul"—he cringed—"Thea. That desert is dangerous under the best of circumstances, you know that. And with ... whatever is plaguing you ..."

"Don't worry," I told him. "I know what I am doing." I stood, but in a moment of madness that I could not have predicted from myself, I fell to my knees before him, pulled his face toward mine, and kissed him, long and soft and full. I could have lost myself in that kiss without a single regret, but it could not be. The taste of salt in my mouth was surely from both of our tears. I was certain now that I knew the pain of the woman in the desert. I pulled away and felt an emptiness that threatened to break me.

"Now, please," I whispered, my hands on his knees, his chest, his cheeks, memorizing every curve and plane of him. "I must go."

This time, I left the palace on foot, led by Orly, with Zav at my side. I had strapped supplies to both his back and mine. I longed for the weight of Eytan's quiver and bow across my shoulders again. Though I could now properly see the palace grounds, the magnificent golden gates, and the city beyond, I barely registered the incredible views or those faces that looked at me, full of curiosity, as we made our way through the city. I felt numb, as if even my vision had been dulled.

At the city gates, I thanked Orly, and I turned my back on Midbar and on Eytan. I knew I would never return.

* *❋* *

CHAPTER TWENTY-THREE

* *❋* *

I walked into the desert, past the village where the old women had saved Eytan's life and mine. I walked until I found a stretch of sand that felt familiar, though it bore no landmarks, no gash in the earth to tell of what had passed beneath. There I sat and waited for nightfall. When the moon appeared in the sky, I took my mother's vial from around my neck. It was dull and empty now; whatever magic had existed within it had now been extinguished. But I hoped it would still call to the woman. I set it upon the sand, in a pool of moonlight, and bid the magic to return. I closed my eyes. I waited.

Perhaps I slept, perhaps I was still sleeping, but when I opened my eyes, I was no longer surrounded by an empty landscape. Instead, I sat in a grove of tall, white trees, their roots nestled impossibly in the unforgiving sand. The forest stretched on as far as I could see in every direction, disappearing over the horizon like a strange white-and-black ocean. The moon did not seem to shine upon the trees but rather to radiate out of them. In the distance, the woman watched me.

"Why have you come?"

I could not even see her lips move at such a distance, but her voice sounded from right beside me, as if she were whispering her words in my ear. Ahead, she made only the tiniest flicker of movement, and then she was at my side. She watched me, waited for me to speak.

"It is you, isn't it? The curse. It's you." There was nothing accusatory in my tone. It was a simple fact. I needed desperately for her to know that I did not blame her.

"Curse," she murmured. It was not a question.

"You said you knew my mother. Do you know ... do you know that she is dead?"

The pain in her face was just like it had been in my dreams. "I felt her go."

Tears pricked my eyes yet again. "So did I." I knelt and retrieved the vial from where it was still nestled in the sand. "She gave me this," I said, "before I left the Wall—my home. It was then that things ... began to change. I saw strange visions, nightmares. I felt her die, though that should not have been possible. Then, on the sea, there was the dream, the water. The vial burned me." I pulled my collar down and showed her the mottled skin of my breast. "And in the desert, when our caravan disappeared, when those warriors attacked us, poisoned us ... it was you, wasn't it? All of it ..." My voice caught in my throat, and then the anger came. "All of it was you."

Again, that anguish. Her face was actually distorted with it, as if my words caused her physical pain. "I never meant ..." She shook her head. "Easier to show you." She reached trembling fingers toward me and raised her eyebrows, asking permission.

I nodded.

Her fingertips settled on my temples, and suddenly I was somewhere else. I was someone else.

I was a young but ancient woman, beautiful, mysterious, shunned. I lived in the heart of a vast forest where the trees were ancient and precious, far from my true home, a home that I had forgotten long ago. The trees were from that home as well. They were not like the others of the forest, the younger trees that radiated out from the forest's center and created the illusion of the ordinary.

I lived alone among my trees, but I did not mind, for this was where I was meant to be. I was their custodian. I had been so for many lifetimes, well past the confines of even my own memory. I did not know when my vigil had begun, or when or why I had brought my trees to this foreign place. There were inklings in my memory of a great threat, of war and many horrible battles, of flames. Perhaps I had brought my trees here to escape from that. But it made no difference. I was here now. My trees were here now. I did not dwell.

I knew that I was not like others, that I was possibly the only one of my kind. And I knew that I could do things others could not do. But my powers were not a conscious choice. They were reflexes, it seemed, instilled in me perhaps to enable me to fulfill my role as guardian. There were some things I could control, small cantrips that I used mostly to pass the time, but also to conceal myself should others wander through my forest. The trees wanted to know the world and to be known, so I let travelers, few though they were, perceive the forest when they stumbled upon it, and was satisfied with their awe. I, however, did not wish to be seen, so I concealed myself from these people—an easy trick—and watched undetected, learned what it was to be whatever they were.

Time passed like this for what might have been dozens of human lifetimes, had I cared to count them. I saw much of the world, even confined as I was to my forest. I saw desperation and loss and lost ways; I saw pain and death both fought against and chosen. I came to understand love and secrets, and to know that which was forbidden. My forest, in a way, became a sanctuary to these people who passed through it, just as I was a sanctuary to the forest itself. Yet still, I was alone, and silent—merely an observer.

Until one day, a young woman entered my forest, her green eyes more vivid than any grass or leaf I had ever seen, and her gaze settled on me, and she saw me. She saw me, though it was impossible for her to see me, and she smiled.

I had learned of smiles, and I thought of them as a gift. I gave her one in return. She told me her name. I told her I had none. That merely made her smile again. I treasured that smile, so kind and sweet and pure. The woman stayed with me there, beneath my trees, for long hours each day, and each departure promised a return.

We spoke of many things, in the tongue I had heard so much of from the travelers in my forest but had never before tasted upon my own lips. I knew another language, and I taught it to her in whisperings beneath the moon that was nearly as pale as her skin but nowhere near as beautiful. I learned the softness of skin and the incomparable joy of hands that fit perfectly in one another's. I learned the sweetness of a kiss. I learned happiness. She told me that what we felt was love, and I knew it to be true.

Soon, my language flowed easily from her tongue, and so did the simpler magics that came with it. With a word, she could set a flower blooming, or make the moonlight shine brighter through silvery leaves. My trees loved her as well as I did. They grew stronger in her presence. I grew stronger too.

But then one day, she came to me with tears in her eyes.

"I am to marry," she told me. The words still ring clear, the pain in her voice carving into me even now. I knew of marriage. Many lovers had spoken sweetly of it in my forest. Few had wept so bitterly at the prospect as my green-eyed love. She told me she was promised to some lesser lord, in a place far away, where trees did not grow. She would sail across a storm-filled sea to a place of sand and harsh sun, and we would be separated.

No, I told her. No. We could still be together. My trees and I had journeyed from our home before, though the memory of how or when was lost to me. But surely, we could do so again. I would take my forest to wherever she dwelled. No marriage or lord could separate us.

I believed this, with all my heart. And my resolve made her believe it as well. But I was wrong. We were both wrong. I knew that truly when the flames came. The flames, and the men. Perhaps my trees saw that this would come to pass. Perhaps they saw the prying eyes that watched, unbeknownst to my love and me, as we met time and again in the months preceding her wedding. But in my happiness, I did not sense those eyes. I did not hide, or conceal the magic that my love and I practiced in those months.

Instead, I taught her to draw water from dry soil, to heal burns upon the skin, to mend the broken wings of birds and the broken branches of trees. I crafted her a vial of moonlight to remember this land by, in case the moon did not shine so brightly or so sweetly where she went next. I thought that she might need these gifts in the sands across the sea. Those who watched thought me a sorceress and thought that I had poisoned the innocent green-eyed maiden with my black arts.

And so, they came, led by her father, with torches for my trees and a poisoned whip for me. They stripped me and they sheared my hair, the black strands of which my love had taught me to brush and plait until I looked half a lady myself. They lashed my naked back as they set my forest alight, and they hurled insults at me like stones, and my magic gathered within me, preparing to defend me or avenge me in ways I could not fathom. And then she was there.

She had seen the smoke from the towers of her father's manor, and she had run to me. She screamed for them to stop, she hauled men away from me with her bare hands, she caught the whip with her own arm as it arched down towards my ruined back once more. I felt her body draped over mine like a shield until they hauled her off of me, still screaming. She screamed as they held her, as I bled, as my trees burned. She screamed her love for me until she could scream no more, until her father took her by the chin and wrenched her face upwards so that her kind eyes met his cruel ones.

"We will purge this evil from you," he told her. As her pain stayed with me, so did those words. "We will quash its source. You will wed, and you will bear many sons, and you will forget this ... this witch ... this forest whore." I had never heard such hate, such disgust.

It was then that my magic poured out of me, in a hot rage I had not known I possessed. It burst from me, inky black and cloying, terrifying to behold, snaking towards that loathsome man, and my love—my love, too good, too kind—shoved her father out of its path. The magic struck her full in the chest instead. And that was the last I saw of my green-eyed lady. The world swam around me, nothing but sick, icy pain. My eyes closed of their own accord. My nostrils and lungs were choked with the stench of dying trees and failure.

When I finally awoke, I was alone. The men were gone, the flames were gone. My forest lay in ruins. My love was lost to me, and something horrible lurked within her, and I knew it was beyond my power to purge it.

I opened my eyes to the forest in the desert, gasping, shaking uncontrollably, retching, the scent of burnt wood in my nostrils and the echoing of screams in my ears. The woman sat before me, hugging herself, looking small and helpless and so very, very lost.

When I finally regained my breath, I crawled to her and took her hands in mine. "My mother," I whispered. "You loved my mother."

She said nothing. There were tears in her eyes, and they fell, pearly white down her cheeks.

Suddenly, all I had known—stories told to me in childhood, offhand remarks by my parents about the past, about my spiteful grandfather, about a wood that had once lived where our manor now stood—all the small truths of my life fell into place, and all was clear.

For my father had told me of his good fortune in winning my mother's hand when she had been too ill to travel across the seas to marry a Midbari lord. But she had not been ill. She had been cursed, suffering from an ailment incurable and eventually fatal, one that stemmed from a love my father could not have understood.

And my mother had told me of my father's kindness in building our manor in the clearing, which had once held a forest very dear to her. He had done it to please his new bride, but I knew now that that clearing, that forest, had belonged to my mother's love. Being there, in the presence of the memories they had shared, had somehow kept the curse at bay. And leaving the Wall, as my poor Julia had unwittingly done, made us vulnerable to the curse's malice. My little sister, only a toddler, had wandered through a gate left open by some thoughtless stable hand, and they found her body floating in a forest stream. But I understood. Drowning may have killed her, but it was the curse that took her life.

"Did my mother give her life for mine?" I asked softly.

The woman nodded once. When she spoke, it was difficult to understand her through the tears that choked her words. "The vial ... held her magic. When you took it from the place where my trees had been, the curse thought you her, and her you ..." She sobbed, and curled in on herself, hugging her arms tightly. "It sought you out but acted not. There was too much of *her* about you."

"Then it is my fault she is dead." I had feared that all along, but saying it aloud nearly destroyed me.

"No. She chose. She must have left that place for the curse to find her. It took her life. But she ... she only bought you time. The curse is powerful, stronger even than its maker." She looked down at her own hands in disgust, then met my gaze. "I tried to die," she told me. "I thought it could put an end to this. But I cannot." Her face contorted into something bitter and hateful. "I cursed my love and her whole house with death, but I am cursed with life."

"I do not think you cursed her," I said softly. "You never meant to curse anyone at all. You could not control the magic. And it was meant for my grandfather, in any case. My mother saved him from it. It should have killed her." I did not know how I knew this, but I was sure it was so. "Was it her magic or her love for you that let her live? Or was it both?"

The woman looked at me, sadness and hope mingling in her eyes. My heart ached for her, and I pulled her into my arms as she wept.

I woke from a dream that was not a dream and found myself across the sands, back at the docks where Eytan and I had first made port in Bahir. I found myself in an empty alley behind some tavern, nestled in Zav's fur, with no memory of leaving the forest in the desert. I whispered my thanks to my mother's love, though she was no longer beside me. She knew what I aimed to do, but the rest of my journey I would have to make on my own.

There was still much I did not understand. Why had the vial sometimes aided me, and sometimes been used against me by the curse? Why could the woman not control her power, if it had lived inside of her for so many lifetimes? But there was much more I did understand now. I understood why my father had built the Wall. I understood his kindness towards a woman who had never loved him the way she had loved something lost to her forever. And I understood my sister's death, and the fear it had instilled in my parents. It was a relief to finally connect the threads of a tapestry that had so long sat fraying, incomplete. And it was a relief to know that I had the power to set things right, after so many years, afraid though I was of what it meant for me.

And so I sought out a beautiful ship that should have instilled fear in me but, somehow, did not. Captain Vered and the *Aliyah* were at port once more, almost as though they had been fated to be there. I bartered for passage back to Gaerwn for myself and Zav, offering up the supplies I had not needed for the journey back across the desert that never was, and offering also my services in the ship's galley. In truth, I think she would have taken me aboard for free. The bag of gold I found hidden within my pack, which Eytan had undoubtedly bestowed upon me, I kept, tied in its satchel around my neck. I would need it later.

This time I was not seasick even once.

* *❋* *

CHAPTER TWENTY-FOUR
* *❋* *

Gaerwn seemed the same as when I had left, but I felt I was much changed. The sights before me did not awe me as they had before, though they were still beautiful. I did not feel intimidated by the strangers I met at the port, or on the trade roads south towards Saberhold, for I was a frightened, sheltered girl no longer. I was a woman with a lion at my side and blades at my waist, and I had learned to fight from the legendary swordsmiths of Oro. Should I hunger, I had learned to hunt from the outlaws of Firth, to forage from Eytan, Prince of Midbar. And should I need comfort along my journey, I had been taught to sing by the monks of the Temple of Song.

This time, when I saw my crest on its flag in Saberhold, I knew a face for my knight, and I could not keep from smiling. I stayed a night in a quiet inn, where people gave Zav—and perhaps me as well—queer looks, and when it was day again, I went to Agatha's shop, a knot of fear in my belly.

She greeted me as if she had known I would come. She embraced me and stroked my hair in a gesture that reminded me painfully of my mother. Then, she held me at arms' length and looked me over approvingly.

"You have learned much," Agatha told me.

"And more."

She smiled, but though her tone suggested jest, her eyes were full of remorse.

"Well, I shan't keep you long. Not this time."

I smiled too.

"Tea?" she asked, and when she had fetched a tray, we settled down to talk.

I told her everything that had happened since our last meeting, what I had learned, and what I planned to do. She nodded slowly, listening without comment or judgment. When I finished speaking, she took my hands in hers.

"You," she said, "are incredibly brave."

I smiled again, this time through tears. "I am frightened."

"And it does not make you any less brave."

I handed Agatha my mother's vial. "I tried to leave it with the woman in the desert, but she would not take it. She wished for me to return it to my mother. But I ... I do not know if I will have the chance."

"Why do you act so swiftly? You are the last one left for the curse to take, are you not?"

I could not explain, not properly. "I feel I *must* act quickly. The curse is tugging at me. It has been since I left the desert. It wants something, and I fear it will not be satisfied with taking me. I have to break it. For good." I looked down at the vial, now resting on Agatha's long fingers. "Perhaps I can bring some peace to all of them. To Julia, and my mother, and her love. Perhaps that is what I am meant to do."

Agatha closed her fingers around the vial. "Perhaps. In any case, I will see to it that this finds its home."

"Thank you," I told her. And I left.

I journeyed for many more days, but I stopped seldom. Zav did not tire easily here in the woodlands, where food and water were in ample supply. And for some reason, I did not feel the need to eat. I barely even slept. I met people along the way, but I spoke to them in a daze. They seemed foreign to me. Everything seemed distant and ephemeral as I neared my fate.

The Wall, though, seemed as real as ever. Realer, even, as if its essence was stronger than the world around it. I could feel it before it even came into view beyond the trees and the rolling hills. As I neared, I made myself stop, despite how it called to me. I found a place I somehow knew to be the border of the long-lost sacred wood and knelt as if in prayer.

"Malek," I said, "Maeve. If you can hear me, I have need of you." The rest I did not speak aloud. It seemed too terrible to say. But I thought the words with purpose and told the twins of Oro my request. I hoped that they heard. I hoped that they could come.

And then I stood, rested a hand on Zav's shoulder to brace myself for what was to come, and walked through the gates of the Wall. I should have been surprised that those gates, always tightly closed, now stood open, but I was not.

The Wall was untouched by time; the manor within stood empty. I had known it would be so. The Wall had kept my mother here, had kept me here, but the only thing keeping my father was his family. He had lost his wife and had every reason to believe me dead as well. I knew he would not stay.

The main doors swung in easily when I pushed them. They had not been locked or barred. Within, my childhood home had been left for spirits and shadows and dust. Paintings and tapestries had been taken from their hangings, leaned against the walls, rolled up or draped with white linens. The furniture, too, was covered in white cloth. They were to keep the dust off, I knew, but they looked like funeral shrouds through the dust motes that danced in the pale sunlight. I touched the railings as I made my way up the grand staircase, memorizing the feel of the cool, dark wood. I had slid down these banisters as a girl, landing upon Zav's back with ease, much to my mother's dismay and my father's chagrin. I ran my fingers along the damp stone walls that lent a chill to the air now that there were no tapestries to insulate against the cold. It was a different sort of chill than the dry cold of desert nights. It felt strange but also familiar, like a sensation I should have known well but could not recall.

I went first to my father's study, an immense room with high ceilings to allow for the baffling amount of shelving built into the walls. The books had been moved, taken perhaps to some new home my father had found for himself. I pictured trains of wagons rattling along, filled to the brim with old tomes, and my father riding alongside, chiding their drivers to steer carefully. He had always loved his books, collected during his merchant days from lands and cultures innumerable. His voice, when he had read to me, had always been sweet and strong, a confident bass that made even the driest histories seem like thrilling adventures. I was glad the books would be spared what was to come.

His bottled ships were gone as well, but in one corner I found a broken mast, built to scale and painted painstakingly by my father's own hand, lying dejected on the floor. I slipped it into my pocket. I would take it with me, wherever I was going next.

Next, I made my way to my mother's chambers. They, too, stood empty. The silk curtains that had once played in the breeze let in through open windows were now gone. I remembered countless games of hide-and-seek in these chambers, making myself small behind those curtains as my mother pretended not to see me through the thin fabric. Later, Julia had joined too, but she always grew lonely and afraid if we hid separately, so I would hold her in my arms as the silk swayed around us. I could remember the way her eyes shone with wonder at the fabric's dance.

Since I had left the Wall, I had thought constantly of the family I had left behind, but in my guilt, I had barely spoken of them. How could I have spent so long with Eytan and never told him of my mother's curtained chambers, of her sweet, high singing voice, of her riddles that would keep me puzzling for hours? How could I have failed to mention my father's booming laugh or his model ships or his gift with horses? How could I have never told him of sweet little Julia, of how quickly she had learned to walk, of how she could nearly speak in full sentences at the tender age of two, of how she had loved crossed buns?

Pain seized my chest, for I knew that now it was too late. He would never know those things. Zav made a mournful sound, and I turned to face him. I could swear he knew what I meant to do.

"Yes," I told him softly. "It is time."

I had considered burning the manor, meaning to leave no trace of the family that had made a home of a prison and a prison of a home. But it seemed wrong after the cruel fire this place had seen in my mother's youth. I would just have to hope instead that Malek and Maeve would do their part. I believed they would. I had felt them listening, when I spoke my prayer, though they made no response. Perhaps I had inherited some of my mother's magic. So I took a last look around the home that I had once felt so trapped by, and guided Zav back the way we had come.

We left the manor together, woman and lion, the oddest of pairs, for the last time. I knelt beside Zav and the pain spread from my chest through my entire body, a weariness I had never known before. I tried to focus only on him, to ignore the loss I felt. I rested my forehead upon his, looking into those eyes of molten gold. I buried my hands in his mane and kissed his velvety nose.

"You know, I've never minded if it seemed strange," I told him. "You are my best friend. I love you." I steeled myself and stood, steering my lion towards the gates of the Wall. I gave him a light slap on the rump. "Now go."

Zav did not budge.

"Go on," I said, more sharply. "You cannot stay with me through this."

He gave a roar of disagreement.

"Oh, *Zav!* Don't you understand?" The tears were flowing now, and I did not attempt to stem them. "You cannot stay here!"

Zav gave a short rumble and, with his eyes locked on mine, sat down.

I laughed in spite of myself. "Oh, you stubborn beast," I said through my tears. He understood perfectly, and he would not leave me. "Well, come on then."

The grounds inside the Wall were vast, large enough for a scullery, kitchens, stables, and a ring for my father's horses, a sizable hedge maze, a few excellent climbing trees, and, most importantly, a rather large pond, so deep I had to submerge myself completely for my feet to touch the bottom. It was the pond I sought now.

I looked at Zav again. "You must get yourself to safety when this is over," I told him. "Do you understand?"

He blinked slowly.

"I shall take that as a yes."

I drew in a deep breath, feeling more afraid than I ever had before. Then, I set my daggers upon the grass, knelt at the shore of the pond I knew so well, and began to gather stones.

When my pockets were full, I smiled once at Zav, though I trembled with fear, and the tears were falling so thickly now I could barely see my lion. And before I could let my fear stop me, I walked into the water.

For I knew, I had known for some time now, how to break the curse. I had known in Midbar, had admitted to it in my letter to Eytan, trusting him not to read it until I was gone, until it was too late to stop me. The curse had begun in the heart of an old wood, where even older trees had once dwelled. The curse had been held at bay there as well. But to die inside that place, while the curse hunted me without, would undo the magic. Even Agatha agreed. It was a sacrifice, mine to make, and I made it willingly.

The water stung my eyes.

I tried to make myself relax. I walked forward, kicking up the sand at the bottom of the pond as I moved further towards its center. My clothes were so very heavy, it was difficult to move. The water felt thicker than it had any right to. But that was all for the best. This was where it would all end. This was where I would finally rest.

My chest was growing tight, my vision beginning to blur. Bubbles escaped through my mouth and nose, small at first, but growing larger as I battled for control of my lungs. Finally, I could help it no longer. The air burst from me, and before I could tell myself not to, I inhaled. Water flooded my lungs. With a sick fascination, I thought, *So, this is how it feels to drown.*

This is how my Julia had felt, how she had suffered. That pained me far more than the aching desperation for air that I now felt. She had been so small, so alone ... she must have been so frightened. My body thrashed without my consent, my hands reaching for the surface. Even outstretched, my arms were not long enough to break through the rippling mirror above me. I was growing weaker from lack of air, and even though I kicked and struggled, the stones in my pockets succeeded in weighing me down. My boots, dress, and cloak did their part as well, sinking with the weight of the water and dragging me down with them.

Good, I thought. *This is right. This is as it must be.*

I could see nothing but blackness now, interspersed with bursts of light in rainbow prisms. I stopped struggling. Somewhere, muffled and far away, I thought I could hear a crumbling sound and the moaning of my lion. Then the sound was gone, all at once, as if all the world had fallen away. I had never heard such silence.

And there was Julia.

She was a toddler no longer. In fact, she looked almost of an age with me. No, that was not quite true. Her cheeks still held the fullness of a babe, the kind that faded away as one grew to adulthood. Her eyes shone, nut-brown like my father's and saucer-wide. Her lips were upturned in the smile I remembered so well. Her hair, the same dark locks as my mother's, hung loose and wild and lovely around her face. She looked like a princess from a story. In a way, I thought, she was.

"Thea," she said, and my heart swelled with joy. The last I had heard her speak my name, she could not even fit the "th" around her baby teeth.

"Julia," I replied, and I was smiling through my tears. She held out her arms to me, and we ran to each other, both laughing, both weeping. I cradled her head to my breast and felt I was home.

"My sister," I whispered. "My sister ..."

Blinding pain filled my chest and blinding light my eyes. Something was pressed to my lips, forcing my mouth open, and then it was gone, replaced once more by that pain in my chest.

Stop, I wanted to say. *Stop. Julia is waiting for me.*

But I could not speak. I was not sure I could even breathe. I could not tell if my eyes were open, or if the harsh light I saw was shining through my eyelids. I could barely feel my body beyond the pain. And then I heard his voice.

"Thea," he pleaded, "stay with me."

I sputtered and coughed and felt a flood of water brimming up from deep in my throat. I managed to roll onto my side as the stream erupted from my lips. Eytan was beside me, cradling my head, patting my back. I could feel grass against my skin. My bare skin. Where were my clothes?

"Cold," I croaked. "Julia ..." I could not manage anything more. Out of the corner of my eye, I thought I saw black wings taking flight, receding into the distance. But when I turned my head to look, there was nothing but sky.

Eytan pulled me into his arms as I shivered and shook. Zav was nuzzling my soaking hair, his warm nose breaking through the icy feeling in my bones. But I could barely acknowledge their presence. Everything seemed too sharp, too pressing, too real. My eyes fought to regain focus. I thought Eytan was weeping. I leaned into his chest and closed my eyes against it all, and I slept.

*****

CHAPTER TWENTY-FIVE

*****

When I awoke, I was clothed once more. I was dry. I was wrapped in warm blankets. I was nestled against Zav's belly, his paws surrounding me protectively. Gingerly, I sat up. I recognized my surroundings. We were still within the Wall, sheltered beneath one of my favorite climbing trees.

But something was different. I gasped, standing unsteadily to better survey the space. We *were* within the Wall, in a manner of speaking, but the Wall was a wall no longer. In every direction, it lay destroyed; shining white rubble spilled upon the ground, almost like snow. I looked towards the manor, the kitchens, the scullery, the stables. They too were gone. Their stones lay in ruins, not unlike Oro. Their wood and straw and anything they had contained within seemed to have disappeared. I could swear that ivy and wildflowers had already begun to grow among the ruins.

"We heard your prayer."

"We did as you asked."

Malek and Maeve came smiling, walking towards me from nowhere, as if they had been there all along, and I simply had not noticed. Perhaps they had been.

"I ... thank you," I said breathlessly. "But ..."

"But you were not meant to see it?" Maeve asked.

"You thought you would be far from this world by now," Malek added.

"Yes."

"I could not let that happen."

I turned and saw Eytan, beautiful and strong, full of concern, walking towards me. He touched my face hesitantly, as if afraid it would crumble beneath his fingers.

"How do you feel?" he asked.

I was suddenly angry. "How did you reach me in time?"

"Luck, partially," Malek offered.

"Luck that he was already on Gaerwn's soil when you called to us," Maeve added. "We sensed him here."

"And we brought him to you," Malek said. His tone was soft. "He needed you."

"I still do," Eytan said. I could hear the pain in his voice.

I felt faint, overwhelmed, and also furious. Being here, within my Wall that was a wall no longer, I felt strangely vulnerable. And I felt that I was meant to be somewhere else now, somewhere far away, and perhaps more beautiful. I pictured my mother and my sister waiting for me there, sad that I had been so close and had left them again.

"You should not have come," I said sharply. The pain that flashed across Eytan's face at my words cut me as well. I softened my tone. "You ... you should not have saved me. I have to die. It is the only way—"

"To break the curse?" Maeve suggested.

"I would not worry about that," said Malek.

Eytan cupped my face in his hands. Tears shone in his perfect dark eyes. "You did die, Thea. Your breath had left you; your body was cold. You were gone."

"Then how ...?"

"I went into the water after you. I ... I had to cut you from your clothes." He blushed furiously, and for a moment, I was just a girl once more, in love with a sweet, handsome boy, and giddy at his shyness. But his expression grew dark as he continued to speak. "I've seen men close to drowning, out at sea. I've seen them brought back, very rarely. I had to try."

"He brought you back, but you *were* gone," Malek said. The curse is broken."

"You succeeded," Maeve added. "Your mother and your sister—"

Malek smiled. "They are at peace."

Maeve stepped forward and kissed me on the forehead. "We must go now."

"Oro awaits us." Malek mirrored his sister's action.

There was so much I wanted to say to them, gratitude I knew not how to convey. But I also had so many questions. I had thought I'd left curiosity behind me, a product of the living world, a world of which I had no longer felt a part since leaving Bahir. But I was curious now. About many things.

The twins seemed to read my thoughts.

"Don't fear," Malek said. "You'll see us again."

"Remember, 'if you ever are in need ...'" Maeve winked.

I grinned. "'Two words will see you safe.'"

The twins returned my smile, and with that, they disappeared into mists that had not been there a moment before, leaving me with my love, the betrayal he felt clear upon his face.

Eytan and I walked the grounds of what had once been my home. In a way, it was beautiful in this state, unburdened by the years of hurt that had once weighed upon it. I, too, felt unburdened, but my relief was mingled with sadness as I remembered all that I had been in this place. That person, that child Thea who had played pranks on the cooks and hidden in the hedge maze to avoid needlepoint lessons, that Thea was dead. She had begun to fade away as soon as she left the Wall, and had eventually drowned, just like her sister, leaving room for ... whoever I was now, whoever I was becoming.

"You should have let me help you," Eytan said finally. He had been silent a long while. I wondered if he had been imagining me inside the Wall. He had known me as a child, I had to remind myself, brief though our meeting back then had been. Could he still picture me as that girl? I barely could.

I sighed. "Eytan," I said. "I love you." I could see how happy the words made him, despite his anger.

"And I you," he told me.

My heart swelled. "And that is why I could not bring you with me. If our roles had been reversed, I would never have let you do what I did. I would have begged; I would have insisted we find another way. And you would have acquiesced. Am I wrong?"

"No," he murmured.

"If you had begged me to live, to find another way, don't you know I would have listened? It would have been the wrong choice, but I would have listened. Because I was afraid. Of dying, yes, but more than that, I was afraid ..." I struggled to keep my tears at bay. "I was afraid of never having the chance to be with you. So, yes, had I told you of my plans, I would have chosen life. I would have chosen *you*. And the curse would have eventually destroyed us both."

Eytan was crying in earnest now, tensing his jaw against the tears that would not stay captive behind his eyes. "When I read that letter, I sent envoys to the desert, hawks to the ports. I had it that a girl and a lion had boarded a ship not a *day* after you left the palace. It should not have been possible ... but it could only have been you. No matter how swiftly I managed to cross the desert, no matter how much the winds were in my favor at sea, you were out of reach. And I knew then that I was too late."

I wiped his tears. "Yet, here we are."

"Yes. Here we are."

There was more to say, so much more, but neither of us had the patience for words. Eytan swept me into his arms, and he kissed me. He kissed me, and I tasted the salt of both our tears for the second time. He kissed me in the ruins of the Wall, and I knew that I was home.

That night, as we slept upon the grass of my childhood home, as I lay safe in Eytan's embrace, I dreamed of the woman.

Perhaps I woke, and she was really there, perched upon the ruins of the Wall, but perhaps it was all in my mind. I decided it did not matter. I slipped out of Eytan's arms and went to her. She was naked, with her back to me. Her wounds were healed. There were barely any traces to show that they had ever been. She did not smile when she turned to face me, but the deep sadness in her eyes had abated.

"You," she said, "are quite extraordinary."

I laughed. "I'm just a girl with a lion."

"And is that not extraordinary? In any case, you are more than that." She held my gaze. "You do realize what I am, yes?"

"I ... I believe so. You are the spirit of the forest. The forest that was here."

"I suppose that is as accurately as it can be said in your language." She smiled then. "The power of that curse is not such to be broken by a mere child. Or a mere human, for that matter. So yes, you are extraordinary. You are, I daresay, your mother's daughter."

I grew sad then. "I thought ... if I broke the curse, you could be with her."

She smiled again, and I could see a ghost of that pain in her eyes. Yet, she seemed at peace. "That is not the way of it, I fear. Not for me." She glanced behind me, to where Eytan slept, still curled around the space where my body had been a moment before. "But it may be for you." She rose from the jagged bit of Wall on which she had made her seat. She came to me in that way she had, where it was difficult to tell if she had actually moved, or if the world around her had shifted to accommodate her wishes. She took my hands in hers, kissed me on the forehead, and disappeared, just as Malek and Maeve had earlier that day. A queer feeling in my stomach told me that was no coincidence.

After she was gone, the mist began to clear. But just before I awoke, I heard her voice once more.

"Thank you."

* *** *

EPILOGUE

* *** *

Eytan and I took our time together, traveling slowly back to the ports north of Saberhold. We finally told each other the things we had been afraid to say before. I told him of my family, silly little stories that left us both smiling, and he told me what it was to be a prince. He told me what our lives would be like together in Midbar. But I was firm in my resolve. Yes, he would return to Midbar. He was a prince, after all, and had an obligation to his people. But I would not go with him. At least, not directly.

I would find my father, tell him of what I had seen and done. I would tell him his wife and daughter were at peace. I would tell him I was sorry. And I would learn what I was as well. For I knew I was more than I seemed. My mother had possessed magic, and I knew now that I possessed it too. It was what had drawn Agatha to me so long ago, what had kept the curse from destroying me the moment I left the Wall. I had felt it stirring in me for a long time now, but fear of the curse had kept me from reaching out for it. I would reach now.

And so, Eytan and I said our farewells. We both felt the pain of it, but it was not forever. I would return to him one day. In the meantime, we both had much to learn.

Zav and I traveled Gaerwn. We went first to my father, who was not difficult to find, and I spent many weeks with him, curled up on the rug of his new study with familiar books and bottled ships and his familiar smile. It brought me such joy to see him smile. He had thought me dead. He had thought he had lost everything. I did not know until then what a gift I was to him. But, eventually, Zav and I had to bid him farewell again. He understood. Now that there was no Wall, no curse, he seemed glad to see me explore the world. Besides, I assured him Zav would keep me safe. My father chuckled at that and told me he was quite sure it was the other way around. My heart swelled at the pride in his voice.

Zav and I made our way to Oro, where Malek and Maeve were waiting. Of course, they knew I was coming. I brought with me a piece of the Wall—a thin, flat slab of the glimmering white stone not much larger than my hand—to remember my past by. I meant to leave it in Oro, as a monument. But when I showed it to Malek and Maeve, they had another idea for it. They made from it a mask, shimmering white, with emerald ivy engraved upon it and protective magic woven within it. They were right to make it, I knew. My mother's story had taught me that there were times when it was better to remain anonymous, and I still had my father to protect. It would not do for the world to know the quest his daughter was on.

Then, as the nameless woman with the golden lion and the ivy mask, I journeyed. I sought old tomes and long-forgotten histories, looking to unravel the mysteries of beings such as Malek and Maeve and the woman whom my mother had loved. I sought people as well, people with gifts far greater than my own, and I learned all I could from them. When I grew lonely, when I missed Eytan so intensely that no letter delivered on Kes's silver wings could bring me comfort, there were outlaws, monks, and swordsmiths who knew me well, and whose doors (and tents) were always open to me.

Word of the masked girl traveled even further than I did. Soon, Eytan's letters held queries about my exploits: Had I truly saved an entire village from a plague and faced a wyvern alone? (I had healed one child from some minor illness; my magic was still only budding. And the wyvern had befriended *me* one day as I collected shells along a stony seashore.) The rumors and legends ranged from truth to fiction to absurdity, and whenever I chuckled at overhearing them in some shadowy corner of an inn's tavern, I wondered if Eytan was hearing them and chuckling as well.

My travels took me to many places that Eytan and I had seen together, and to many more I had never known existed. And, eventually, they took me back across the sea. By then, I was called the Lion Girl, known for my beastly companion and my mysterious white mask.

I returned to Bahir, my mask on my face, my crystal blades at my hips, and Zav at my side. The city gates were open to me, and so were the palace gates beyond them. My feet recalled the way.

And there he was, clad in white, walking with a state official.

"My prince," I called to him. He turned and knew me at once. He approached me slowly, like he was unsure whether I was truly there. I must have looked a mirage, there amidst the sand.

"I have traveled long," I told him, "and bring tidings from old friends. I thought we might sit together and—" I stopped, my breath caught in my throat as he neared me. Seeing him again made me almost giddy.

Eytan stood before me, so close I could smell spices and sweat on him, and pulled the mask from my face. And before he could speak, before I could think to hesitate, my arms were around him, and I was kissing him.

"Thea," he said, his lips still brushing mine. My name sounded like music when he spoke it. It sounded like coming home. "Or should I call you 'Lion Girl'?" We smiled, our lips still pressed against one another's, sharing our laughter like a secret. He brushed a hand through my windblown hair. "So, have you come home, then?"

I kissed him again. "Yes," I whispered. "Yes." I was home.

ACKNOWLEDGMENTS

This book has been a labor of love, but a labor nonetheless. It would not have been possible without the support of my family, friends, editors, and designers.

To Caitlin O'Connell, my editor and dear, dear friend, thank you for being with me every step of the way. From reading my rambling plot ideas (each of which was at least a novella in its own right) over instant messenger to editing the novel once it was at least somewhat book-shaped, you've been such a huge part of this process. But more than that, you've been such a huge part of my life. I am incredibly lucky to call you my friend.

To my husband Seyeol, who sat with me while I wrote in at least a dozen coffee shops across at least four countries, who listened to me puzzle out plot points and character development endlessly, and who read the book even though it's not in your native language, you are my whole heart. Thank you for always encouraging me and for never doubting that I would succeed. 고맙습니다 내 사랑.

To Paul Singer, my dad, who read more drafts of this book than anyone—how are you not sick of it?! Thank you for always being enthusiastic about my stories and begging me for more. You're a big part of the reason this book actually got written.

To both my parents, Paul and Jennifer Singer, thank you for instilling in me a passion for reading and stories. Dad, I wouldn't be the reader, the writer, or the person I am today without you reading *The Lord of the Rings* and *David and the Phoenix* out loud to me when I was little. Mom, I still remember the summer reading charts you made for us in elementary school. You made reading exciting. I would never have become a writer if you hadn't taught me to love stories, and I wouldn't have the skills I do if you hadn't encouraged me to read so widely.

To Ellie, my Bumblebee, thank you for, well, everything. Thea never really got to know her sister, but I can't imagine not knowing you. You are the cleverest, funniest, toughest person I know. Thank you for always making me laugh. Thank you for always being in my corner. Thank you for being my sister.

To S.G. Prince, thank you for guiding me through the indie publishing process and for being so supportive. You've taught me so much, and I don't think I could have figured all of this out without your help!

A huge thank you to Lena Yang for the stunning cover design and the interior design, to Sohini Ghose, my proofreader, for catching even the most minuscule mistakes, and to Angie Isaacs for making me such a gorgeous website!

And finally, to you. Thank you for taking this journey with Thea, Zav, and Eytan, and with me. I wish you many more adventures.

ABOUT THE AUTHOR

Photo by Jennae Lee Photography

Sarah Jane Singer lives in Syracuse, NY, with her four cats and an enviable collection of Funko Pops. She loves creating rich fantasy worlds with unexpected twists and undertones of horror. When she is not writing, she can be found editing, reading tarot, and cooing at bees in her backyard.

CPSIA information can be obtained
at www.ICGtesting.com
Printed in the USA
LVHW10195925022
709187LV00005BA/369